COMFORT HERSELF

D1387595

ABOUT THE AUTHOR

Geraldine Kaye was born in Watford, Hertfordshire in 1925. After serving in the Women's Royal Navy she took a degree in Economics at London University and then worked as a writer and teacher in Malaysia and Singapore. She now lives in Bristol. Her many books for children include *The Rotten Old Car*, *Penny Black* and *Nowhere to Stop*.

GERALDINE KAYE

Comfort Herself

HEINEMANN
NEW WINDMILLS

Heinemann Educational Books Ltd
Halley Court, Jordan Hill, Oxford OX2 8EJ
OXFORD   LONDON   EDINBURGH
MADRID   ATHENS   BOLOGNA   PARIS
MELBOURNE   SYDNEY   AUCKLAND
IBADAN   NAIROBI   HARARE   GABORONE
SINGAPORE   TOKYO   PORTSMOUTH NH (USA)

ISBN 0 435 12315 7

First published 1984 by André Deutsch Ltd
105 Great Russell Street, London WC1
Text Copyright © 1984 Geraldine Kaye
Illustrations copyright © 1984 Jennifer Northway
All rights reserved
First published New Windmill Series 1987

94 13 12 11 10 9 8 7 6

Illustrated by Jennifer Northway

Cover illustration by Andrew Aloof

Printed in England by Clays Ltd, St Ives plc

To
Clare, Elaine, Janet, Kate,
Nola and Sue

1

Comfort Jones was running. She had never run as fast as this or as far, she hadn't known she could. Right across Kensington Gardens and up the Broad Walk with the carrier bag of shopping banging against her legs and her breath scraping in her throat as if she had swallowed barbed wire. She passed Kensington Palace but she didn't see the slivers of brown brick and white paint between the green trees. She didn't even see the Round Pond on the other side like a mirror dropped in the grass. She ran right through a flock of pigeons feeding on the path.

'Take care now, take care,' the old lady said sharply, throwing out handfuls of white bread. She had bought a whole loaf as a Saturday treat. 'Children nowadays, not a scrap of manners.'

But Comfort didn't hear the old lady, only the slap of her own sandals on the asphalt path and the flutter of wings in her face as the pigeons rose in a grey cloud round her. When she reached the Bayswater Road and the busy traffic, she turned along the pavement and ran on. There were paintings hung along the railings, and Margaret always stopped to look, it was only polite when people tried so hard, but Comfort didn't stop.

'Nice ripe peaches eight pence each or three for

twenty,' Jim shouted from his barrow at the corner of
Bell Place as Comfort ran past. 'What's the blooming
hurry, girl? Ants in your pants?'

Comfort was there now. Home. Her white socks

flicked like rabbit scuts as she ran up the steps and took the front-door key out of Margaret's red handbag.

It was dark in the hall after the sunlight. The smell of new polish stung in her chest as she gasped for breath and the brown lino gleamed like a pool in a forest. Mrs Mace leaned from the basement stairs as the front door slammed.

'Oh, it's you, Comfort, it's your mum I was wanting, dear,' she jerked her head at the green rent book on the hall table. 'Just coming is she?' Comfort didn't answer, but she opened the handbag again and pulled several five pound notes from the beige pay envelope in the back pocket. 'Oh, never you mind about that, child,' Mrs Mace said embarrassed. 'You shouldn't be bothering with money at your age.' But paying the rent wasn't the bother, Comfort thought, the bother was the way the notes slid out of her hand and floated away across the floor like blue and white petals, the bother was the way the metal jaws of the handbag snapped at her fingers like a crocodile.

'My goodness me, you're all out of puff,' Mrs Mace said picking up the notes. 'Are you all right, Comfort?' Comfort ran up the stairs and opened the flat door and slammed it behind her. Mrs Mace knocked. 'Whatever is the matter, dearie? Surely you can tell me, Comfort? Where's your mum, Comfort?'

But presently she went away and the flat was quiet.

The cat, Ginger, lay on her bed where they had left him earlier that morning. Everything was just as they had left it. The line of birthday cards on the mantelpiece, the mug of tea by the bed, Margaret's flimsy nightie screwed up like a grape skin. Half a packet of custard creams. And now she was home, Comfort couldn't quite think what to do. She wanted to go back, have a second chance. If she could start Saturday again she could make it right. She pulled the blue dressing-gown on over her tee-shirt and jeans. Her teeth were chattering but the cat was warm, lying like an orange jewel in the setting of her arms.

She had lain like that early in the morning with bright June sunshine streaming through the windows. Even before she opened her eyes, she had known from the sounds outside that it was Saturday. Comfort had never lived anywhere else and that morning the myriad city sounds, the song of London, had seemed like a lullaby, cradled as she was in Bell Place, the nicest flat they had had so far.

Margaret had been fast asleep then – Comfort had always called her mother Margaret – her fair hair fanned out across the pillow. Comfort had sighed gustily hoping to wake her. Bell Place was *called* a flat but it was just one large room really with a kitchen-cum-bathroom behind a frosted glass partition at the end. There were windows from floor to ceiling and curtains with pink and white roses as big as cabbages. How wonderful to find *real* roses as big as that! Outside the windows was a wrought-iron veranda, white like lace against the green leaves of the plane tree which kept itself clean in the city by shedding its bark, a very adaptable tree. Everything had to be adaptable to survive nowadays, Margaret said.

Usually they moved about every three months and Comfort *was* adaptable. They had lived in more rooms, bed-sitters, flats in Hammersmith and Shepherds Bush and Brixton than she could remember. Sometimes they

moved because Margaret changed her job and sometimes because there was trouble with the landlady and
her rules. There had been no trouble with Mrs Mace,
who lived in the basement with her son, Graham, in
heating and lighting, and Ginger. They could have the
flat and welcome, Mrs Mace had said that first day, but
no visitors please, she couldn't be doing with people up
and down on her brand new stair carpet. Margaret had
agreed no visitors because Mrs Mace liked Comfort, had
taken to her from the start. Not everybody did.

Once they had fixed a flat on the phone and gone there
in a taxi with the two suitcases on a cold wet night. The
front door had looked green as GO in the streetlight but
then it had opened and the landlady had looked at
Comfort and the line of her mouth had zipped tight
together like a purse. She was sorry but there was some
mistake and the flat was already taken. They had had to
get back in the taxi and go to the squat where Ruby and
Ferdy lived. Comfort had been smaller then and she
hadn't understood. She understood now.

Comfort got out of bed in her pyjamas, quietly at first
because of not waking Margaret, and then not so quietly
because she was tired of being on her own. She clanked
the kettle against the tap and while it boiled, let Ginger
in and got orange juice for herself and milk for him and
slammed the fridge door and turned on the transistor.

'Oh, Comfort, *please*,' Margaret moaned and turned
over. 'Whatever time is it?'

'Late,' said Comfort swooshing the tea-bag round and
round and then putting the mug on the bedside table.

'Thank you, my lovely. How should I manage without
you?' Margaret said yawning and pulling herself onto
her elbow in her mauve nightie. 'Fortunately I don't

11

have to. Give us the biscuits, will you?'

'I thought you were supposed to be slimming,' Comfort said.

'If a little Margaret is nice, a lot of Margaret must be nicer?' Margaret suggested and added, as Comfort slid into the bed beside her, 'What's this cupboard love in aid of? I thought you were supposed to be eleven, Comfort Jones?'

'Eleven is only eleven,' Comfort said.

'Eleven is grown-up practically,' Margaret said smiling at them both in the dressing-table mirror. The packet rustled and custard cream crumbs sprinkled onto Comfort's hair and hung like dew drops. 'Some people have made their fortunes by eleven.'

'Like who?' said Comfort but she smiled, too, because

Margaret always teased and she really was beautiful. Hair like silver sand which hung round her shoulder in a shining curtain and eyes as blue and innocent as two angel fish but best of all she was always smiling, laughing. When anything went wrong which was quite often, Margaret just shrugged and laughed.

It was no wonder Margaret had so many friends because she made every day a party. Everywhere else they had lived friends had come to see Margaret and stayed and stayed and talked and talked with Margaret saying Hush and Shush until she forgot. Friends used all the milk for their coffee, so there wasn't any in the morning for cornflakes and sometimes no cornflakes either. No visitors was another reason why Bell Place was best.

'Do you think I look at all like you?' Comfort said wrinkling her nose at herself in the mirror. Her skin was pale brown, the colour of acorns somebody said at school, more like Nescafé somebody else said or new potatoes. Her eyes were deep black and her hair was thick and springy round her head and she had neat little ears and tiny gold earrings. Some schools didn't like earrings. Lot of silly nonsense, Margaret said when they sent notes home, but Comfort had had to leave one school because of the earrings.

'Well I hope not, you poor little thing,' Margaret said rustling for another custard cream. 'I mean you're twice as sensible and three times as clever. Course your father was clever, clever as a load of monkeys, brilliant and tricky too, Mante.' She said it softly, lovingly it seemed and Comfort kept quite still because Margaret never talked about Mante. There was no card from Mante. 'He's quite an important person in Ghana.'

'Did you tell him about the scholarship?'

'No need to tell him,' Margaret said. 'Mante knows any child of his would be an egg-head, brilliant. You'll make brain surgeon shouldn't wonder, Comfort Jones, you've got a long way to go.'

'Let's play our game? Let's talk about our house?' Comfort said. 'You go first.' They often played the game on Saturday morning. After the green door shut them out that night, Margaret had started saving a bit each month. A house of your own was the best thing in the world, Margaret said.

'Well, I'm sick of flats,' Margaret's hand slid towards the custard creams. 'What about an old terraced house with lots of bedrooms?'

'I'd rather have a small house,' Comfort said; with lots of bedrooms friends would never go. 'A small house with one bedroom each and just enough garden for a cat?' she added as Ginger paced across her purring and flexing his claws. 'Ouch!'

'As many cats as you like, Comfort, my little Comfort,' Margaret said kissing her. 'Black cats, tabby cats, white cats.'

'That's six biscuits,' Comfort said. 'You've got no backbone, like Granny said. And your new skirt won't fit.'

'My sensible daughter, how come I have such a sensible daughter, beats me?' Margaret said.

'I'm a throw-back to Granny, she's sensible, isn't she?' Comfort said wondering, thinking of the house in Harrogate, gleaming silver, clean duster every day and lavender smelling polish. But of course Granny and Grandad didn't live in Harrogate now.

'Your granny is eminently sensible,' Margaret said but

her voice seemed to mean something else. 'Come on, time to get up.' She flung back the duvet and jumped up pulling on her jeans and the flowery, silky smock she had bought in the Portobello Road last week. White lilies, pink tulips, yellow daffodils. 'Breakfast first, shopping second and zoo third, okay?'

'Can we do the shopping in Kensington High Street,' Comfort said. There were not so many friends in Kensington High Street. Not quite so many.

'Anything you like,' Margaret said.

Half an hour later Comfort skipped down the front steps.

'Nice morning. Nice ripe peaches,' Jim said with a wink as he set up his barrow on the corner.

'Peaches? Can we?' Comfort said but Notting Hill was busy with people and already Margaret was waving. Kensington High Street was almost as busy and the waving went on and it was Comfort who pushed the trolley round the supermarket, getting things off the shelves, thinking of Sunday dinner and Monday tea. She worked things out better than Margaret. 'We are *going* to the zoo, aren't we?' Comfort said.

'Of course we are, lovey,' Margaret said dropping chocolate biscuits into the trolley. 'Didn't I promise?' But people were calling out, 'Oh Margaret, long time no see?' And the silk smock rippled as she waved back and it hardly seemed fair to *make* her go to the zoo.

'Ferdy's having a party at his place,' Margaret said as they reached the check-out. 'I've said we'll just look in for a minute. Settle up, will you, darling?' She gave Comfort the red handbag and Comfort counted out the money and packed the shopping and walked out to the pavement.

Lilies and tulips and daffodils flashed in the sun as Margaret ran. There was a screech of brakes and then a crash like a hundred dustbin lids all dropped at once. And then silence.

Comfort blinked. The pavement was very bright after the shop and she couldn't seem to see much. Only people running and a bus half on the pavement the other side and flowers spilled across the road.

The ambulance cut through the crowd like a white tooth.

At the hospital Comfort sat on a chair. Through the swinging door she could see a screen and people in white coats hurrying, whispering. 'Watch that heart.'

Comfort sat quite still. Her thoughts had flown away like birds and her head was empty. She didn't know how long she had been there but it must be a long time because the cup of tea was cold and scummy at her feet and nobody was hurrying any more.

'There's a child, isn't there?' somebody said.

'Where?'

Comfort picked up the shopping and the red handbag and ran down the corridor and out of the swing doors and across the car park. Right across Kensington Gardens. Right back to Bell Place.

'Comfort, Comfort?' A voice was calling from the pavement outside. Ferdy's voice, his party must be over. Where had the afternoon gone, Comfort wondered. The sky above the trees was streaked with pink and birds were chirruping in the plane tree just like an ordinary evening. Comfort blew gently into Ginger's fur making pale rosettes in the orange brightness.

'Comfort, Comfort?' Ferdy called again intrusive as a cuckoo. She waited until he had gone and then shut the window and bolted it. She bolted the flat door, too, because Mrs Mace had a key. Margaret had put a bolt on and the screw heads stuck out like little gold mushrooms.

There were sounds in the house now. Whispering and the creak of stairs.

'Comfort, oh Comfort, dear, please open the door. Comfort, are you all right?' Mrs Mace's voice was quavery, her key turned in the lock and the gold screws rattled in their sockets but the bolt held.

It was quiet again after that. As if the house was holding its breath, wondering what was going to happen. A different voice said, 'Comfort, dear, this is Miss Hanker, Jenny Hanker, I'm a social worker from the children's department. Please won't you open the door? Comfort, are you there?'

'She's bolted it on the inside, must have, the little madam,' Mrs Mace whispered. 'They will put these bolts, quite spoils the paintwork. Tell you what I'll do.'

Comfort pulled the suitcase down from the wardrobe, the striped one was hers with her initials, C.J. It was time to go. Outside there was a ringing sound as Mrs Mace banged the cat food tin against his plate. Ginger jumped off the bed and scratched at the door and circled and mewed.

There were five people on the stairs, Mrs Mace and her son Graham, Ferdy and Ruby and Miss Hanker, and as Comfort opened the door their faces turned towards her like sunflowers turning to the sun. Mrs Mace's face quivered and crumpled and Ferdy's eyes shone black and wet. They looked scared, Comfort thought, as if something terrible had happened. The most terrible thing that could happen.

'Comfort?' somebody whispered.

Comfort decided to let herself know then what she had really known for a long time. That Margaret had been knocked down by a bus that sunny Saturday morning. That Margaret was dead.

2

White faces, brown faces, squeals of laughter and the tock of ping-pong balls. A faint smell of stew.

'I've got to see if Miss Hanker's come yet,' Comfort murmured slipping out of the common room of Ivyside Court. Across the hall was a line of canvas chairs under the window where children often sat watching and waiting for visitors. Behind them net curtains obscured the shiny green of the laurel bushes and the street beyond like a veil of mist. It seemed to Comfort that something of the same kind, a veil of mist, lay between her and everything at Ivyside Court. Between her and the rest of the world. She could not see the way ahead.

She knew she was in care under Section 2 of the Children's Act of 1980. Miss Hanker believed it right to be as precise and straightforward as possible with a child as strong and resilient as Comfort. And Comfort knew anyway about going into care; her friend, Carmen, had gone into care when her mother was ill. It was a sort of waiting while things were decided, a sort of limbo.

Everyone was kind, Horlicks-kind, second-helping kind and if the other children avoided the place next to hers at meals, eyes sliding away narrow as half-moons, Comfort could understand that. Her grief was embarrassing. They might have liked it better if she cried, then they could be sorry, put their arms round her neck and give her sweets. But Comfort didn't cry. What was the use of crying which only made your head ache and stuffed up your nose? You had to be adaptable to survive nowadays, Margaret said, and Comfort was adaptable, Comfort was a survivor.

The sound of the ping-pong ball came from behind the heavy mahogany door and then a burst of laughter from Uncle Dick. 'Game to me, another game to me.' It would be all right to sit on the chairs and wait for Miss Hanker, Comfort thought. But Uncle Dick and Auntie Phyllis didn't like anybody being on their own, *brooding* they called it. 'Where am I going after this?' Comfort had asked Uncle Dick the day before. 'What a worry-guts it is!' Uncle Dick said cheerfully. 'Let us do the worrying, Comfort, that's what we're here for.'

Comfort crept up the stairs, though going up to her bedroom during the day was definitely not all right. At Ivyside Court it was all rules and bells and doing what other people told you. Comfort was put in with Peggy, each had a bed with a pink candlewick bedspread and a white chest of drawers, and they shared the large white wardrobe.

Peggy had been asleep in the next bed with her long fair hair spreading across the pillow like a mermaid's when Comfort arrived and was helped into bed by Auntie Phyllis the first night with hot milk and a white pill. But Peggy was sitting up in bed when Comfort woke next morning. 'Do you ever take your earrings off? I bet they're never real gold,' Peggy said. 'Ever so sorry about your mum, I cried my eyes out when I heard about your mum.' It was only polite to say something, only manners and Comfort should say something back. But Comfort said nothing.

20

'Where did they dig up a name like *Comfort*?' Peggy said after a bit.

'From my father,' Comfort said. 'It's quite common in Ghana.' After breakfast she had hidden the red handbag. It was the way Peggy's eyes sort of licked and licked at her earrings, wanting them so much. You should be sorry for people who stole things, Margaret said, which was all very well.

The large white wardrobe creaked.

Comfort took her diary from her top drawer and flicked back through the pages. Granny had given her a five year diary when she was eight and she had kept it ever since, she had been to fourteen schools since the diary started. Some days she only wrote 'Steak and kidney pie,' or 'Miss Trilby bad-mooded,' but seeing the words she could remember that day.

Miss Trilby had been so pleased when Comfort won the scholarship. 'One of the best schools in England, one of the oldest,' her fervent whisper had been flavoured with the violet cachous she always chewed and her eyes were bright as topaz. 'I'm proud of you, Comfort, the whole school is proud.' At morning assembly everyone had clapped but Margaret has seen things differently as she often did. 'A lot of old-fashioned snobbish nonsense,' she had said. 'Tokenism, that's what it is. I'm not having my child put through the mill of some half-baked public school just because she's bright. Comfort's going to Holland Park like everybody else.' Standing beside her, Comfort had seen Miss Trilby's eyes fade back to their usual puddle-grey, and had felt something fade inside herself.

The large white wardrobe creaked again.

'What is going to happen to me?' Comfort wrote

pressing hard. It was June 25th now. 'I don't like sharing with Peggy all that much.' Peggy whirled and twirled as she talked. Her mother was a dancer and she was going to be a dancer too and you had to start pushing up the ladder as soon as you could, Peggy said. 'Why can't I stay at Bell Place?' There was money in the red handbag for the rent and she could draw her own child allowance and buy her own food and go to school every day. 'They never let children do what they want.'

But was it what she really wanted.

'Mante,' Comfort whispered thinking of a time before the diary. Mante's hand on the push-chair, the shout of his laugh, his coughing at night, Mante had hated the London winter. Voices raised and the slam of the front door and then silence. Comfort coughed a lot in the winter too. There had been birthday cards from Carmen and Ferdy and Addie and Granny and Grandad but no card from Mante this year or last. Mante had forgotten. 'Mante.'

There was a spurt of laughter and the wardrobe rattled and shook and a second later Peggy flung back the door and stepped out wearing Comfort's best green dress and an air of exaggerated gaiety. 'Is that a spell or something, don't you go putting your spooky old spells on me, Comfort Jones.'

'I don't know any spells,' Comfort said, her fingers starting on a secret journey behind her back. Peggy had been alone in the bedroom with the red handbag for goodness knows how long.

'Bet you do, you're good at spells and voodoo magic, all you lot,' Peggy said twirling in front of the mirror so the green skirt flew out in a circle. 'Anyway, you shouldn't be up here day-time, it's not allowed.'

'I know,' said Comfort and feeling the cold clasp of the handbag safe and undiscovered in its place, she added more boldly, 'neither should you.'

'Don't you go telling, you don't catch *me* telling,' Peggy said flicking her fair hair back over her shoulders and spinning like a top, this time there were two circles flying out round her, one fair and one green. 'Anyway Auntie Phyllis lets me do things because I've been here longer than anybody else, so there. And you needn't think *anything* because I was just trying your dress on, that's all. You don't catch me nicking people's things, so there. Anyway green's unlucky.' She looked at herself in the wardrobe mirror and then stared resentfully at Comfort. 'You're spoilt, you are, all the lovely things you got, spoilt. When did you get this dress?'

'Four weeks ago,' Comfort said thinking of that after-noon, window-shopping. 'I like that green dress,' she had said. She should have known better because Margaret bought it right out of Harrods window and never mind the rest of the week.

'It doesn't suit me, does it?' Peggy said pulling it off. 'Anyway what did you want to come up here for?'

'I wanted to be by myself,' Comfort said staring at the poster of a baby seal on the opposite wall. SAVE OUR SEALS. She didn't care about her green dress but the baby seal helpless on the icefloe, seemed unbearably pathetic and her eyes filled with tears. 'I wanted to write my diary.'

'Pardon me for breathing,' Peggy said pulling her tee-shirt over her head. 'Sweet isn't he?' she said follow-ing the direction of Comfort's eyes. 'Wouldn't mind having his coat, mind, makes a lovely coat, baby seal. My mum's going to get me pretty things like you got. She's a dancer, well it's actress really, only it's getting the right parts, know what I mean?' she added slipping into her mother's tone of voice. 'She's going after this job in Birmingham and if she gets it she's going to get a flat up there for me and her. I'm not stopping here for ever, so you needn't think it.' She whirled round suddenly angry. 'Where are you going, then?'

'I don't know,' said Comfort. Peggy made up her own life, worked it out like a fairy story, telling lies some people would call it, but at least she knew what she wanted.

'You ought to ask your social worker, that's what she's paid for, isn't it?' Peggy said in an experienced tone. 'You want to ask her where you're going pretty quick because you can't stop here. That's Annabel's bed and

she'll be back from hospital soon as they've done her tonsils and she'll want her own bed, won't she?'

'Annabel?' Comfort said twisting the tufts of pink candlewick in her fingers. Suddenly the bed itself seemed flimsy, an undulating raft on an endless, boundless sea.

'Well it wouldn't be right you having her bed, would it, I mean you don't really belong in England even. Why don't you go back where you came from?'

'I didn't *come from* anywhere,' Comfort mumbled. Why don't you go back where you came from? How long are you stopping? It was something people said, kids in the playground, strangers in the street even. A cruel joke. It was just ignorance made people mean, Margaret said, which was all very well.

'Africa?' Peggy said, her eyes naughty-bright. 'It's your roots. That's where you ought to go to, Africa.'

'Africa?' But it was so long since she had heard from Mante, she hadn't got his address, Miss Hanker was trying to get in touch.

'I quite fancy these boots, mind, smashing,' Peggy said plunging back into the wardrobe like a diver after treasure. They were white boots with fringes round the top. 'Give us a go with your boots.' She pushed her feet into them and danced across the bedroom. 'What'll you swap for these boots, eh? She's never going to let you wear them is she, Auntie Phyllis, even if they do let you stop. Just like to see what they say down stairs, their eyes'll pop out when they see these boots.'

Comfort listened to the white boots thumping down the stairs and crossing the hall, the door of the common room opened and closed. Downstairs the front-door bell rang.

'Comfort, Comfort,' Auntie Phyllis called from the hall. 'Where ever has the child got to?'

'Here,' said Comfort.

'Hallo, Comfort,' Miss Hanker said. 'How are you?'

'All right,' said Comfort. It was just the pattern of her life was gone and she couldn't see the way ahead. Once

26

she had taken a kaleidoscope to pieces, searching for its magic, and found instead a few fragments of coloured foil and some bits of mirror.

'I've just come from Bell Place,' Miss Hanker said as they settled in the line of chairs under the window. 'Did your mother keep things in a special place? I can't find any papers, nothing but clothes, no letters even?' She was unable to keep a note of reproach out of her voice because such a lack of proper documents did complicate her task enormously.

'She didn't keep letters,' Comfort said staring out of the window. 'She threw letters and things away straight after she read them. If it was important she would remember, that's what she said. She said people drowned themselves with bits of paper.' Comfort smiled apologetically because she knew such an attitude was eccentric. Lots of people had disapproved of it, Miss Trilby, for instance, and Comfort herself hadn't always liked it because it wasn't just papers. There was the doll's house. 'You have to travel light in this life,' Margaret had said leaving it behind the move before the move before last. Was it still there in the cupboard at Shepherds Bush?

'It's a point of view, I suppose,' Miss Hanker said with a sigh. If people were trained as infants to keep their papers in good order, it could save millions of pounds spent searching through records. 'I can't find any marriage certificate or your birth certificate even. And you've no idea of your father's address?'

Comfort shook her head. Mante had got a new house in a new place and a new wife called Efua now. 'Maybe we could phone him up?' she said. 'Ask directory inquiries?' Hadn't Margaret phoned up friends in America just when she felt like it. Mante would be so marvellously surprised.

'Tch, tch, how can you phone up somebody called Jones in a foreign country when you don't know their address?' Miss Hanker said. How ironic, she thought, that a child as exotic as Comfort should have a name like Jones. 'What about other relations, your mother's family, did she have brothers or sisters for instance?'

'There's Granny and Grandad,' Comfort said carefully. You had to be careful what you told people, what you gave away couldn't be taken back. Since the flat with the green front-door even Comfort's smile was careful. 'They used to live in Harrogate but they live in Kent now. Smithy Cottage, Penfold, Kent.'

'Why ever didn't you tell me?' Miss Hanker said but she smiled forgivingly because at least she had something to work on. 'What a funny girl you are, forgetting your own granny and grandad.'

'I didn't forget,' Comfort said.

As soon as Miss Hanker had gone Comfort went back to the bedroom. The red handbag was scarlet and smooth, she opened the clasp, sniffing the Margaret smell, her essence trapped there but growing ever fainter, piling the contents on the bed. The beige envelope, the pay packet, still had ten pound notes and one pound notes, sixty pounds in all and a small purse of coins. Mauve and pink eye-shadow, a dry-cleaning ticket, a green cinema ticket and something else right at the bottom of the back pocket, a sausage of blue paper, an airmail letter rolled up small.

Comfort's throat felt tight and her hands were shaking as she unfolded it, as if she was doing something wrong. But the only wrong thing was being up in the bedroom during the day and that was only Ivyside Court wrong. The letter was from Mante and addressed to Margaret Kwatey-Jones in the flat at Brixton.

'Kwatey-Jones,' Comfort murmured softly. When had Margaret dropped the Kwatey, even at the nursery she had been just Comfort Jones. The letter had been written eight years before and Comfort's eyes skimmed quickly, looking for her own name. 'As for Comfort, it would be better if she came out to Ghana where she belongs. My mother and sisters will take care of her for the time being. As you know such family arrangements are common here and Comfort is Ghanaian after all. A child gets her blood from her mother but her spirit comes from her father. I will send her ticket as soon as I can.'

'A child gets her blood from her mother but her spirit comes from her father,' Comfort murmured to herself. She hardly knew what it meant but a strange excitement fluttered in the pit of her stomach and then spread through her whole body. As if her spirit was singing.

Comfort Jones you have a long way to go.

Comfort Kwatey-Jones.

Now she knew what she had to do. She had to write to Mante but it would be better not to tell anybody, Comfort thought, especially Miss Hanker who had been so pleased to find out about Granny and Grandad.

3

'I expect you'll find Granny fusses a bit,' Miss Hanker said carefully negotiating a bus drawing into a bus stop in the narrow lane. So much depended on the initial meeting, she thought, a sullen expression could ruin the most promising placement. The Bartons were family of course but Comfort's colour could be a difficulty. 'Older people do fuss rather. It's a way of being fond of people, fussing. You want the people you are fond of to be quite perfect. You'll have to try to understand that, Comfort. Lots of *Please* and *Thankyou* and perhaps you'll help your granny all you can because she's not very strong.'

'Yes,' said Comfort thinking of Ivyside Court. String-coloured carpet and the smell of disinfectant and a different pudding every day, the poster of the baby seal and the ping-pong table which she hadn't even played on and never would now. At the last glimpse Peggy and Auntie Phyllis had been standing in a clump at the top of the steps with everybody else, nineteen arms waving like an anemone in a rock pool. Comfort had realised then that if she didn't exactly *like* Ivyside Court, she had got quite used to it. She was glad she had let Peggy keep the white fringed boots.

'I *was* going to Holland Park School,' Comfort said, homesick already for London. They had been to a new

pupils' day. HOLLAND PARK SCHOOL IS INTER-
NATIONAL was written at the side, each letter painted
with pictures, children doing different things, children from
different places. 'Couldn't I stay with Mrs Mace?'

'How could you possibly?' Miss Hanker said. Comfort
stared out of the window. Soon there were no more shops
and crowded pavements, only lanes with orchards on
either side, trees with little green apples the size of
marbles, standing in regimented lines like a school
assembly and so much sky it made you feel all small and
cold. Once she and Margaret had gone to the country on
a Sunday to get tadpoles for the school tank. Crossing
wet fields and dragging the jar through a muddy pond
and then running back as fast as they could. In the
country there was so much silence.

'How long am I stopping?' Comfort said suggesting
that the matter wasn't finally decided. It was two and a
half years since she had seen Granny and Grandad and
that Christmas something had happened. Tea-time on
Boxing Day and the tiny sledge and reindeer poised on
the steep cliff of Granny's Christmas cake. Granny had
said Comfort could have the reindeer for herself when the
knife got there and it almost had. But suddenly Margaret
and Granny were quarrelling, shouting in the kitchen
awful unforgivable things. 'Tch, tch, what about the
child, "little pitchers have big ears?" ' Grandad said but
nobody took any notice of Grandad.

'Well, forever I expect, until you're grown up that is,
it's your home now, Comfort,' Miss Hanker said. She
had tried to find the father through the police but there
had been no contact for years. 'I do hope you'll try and
settle. I think we're almost there,' she added smiling out
of the window. 'Isn't it a pretty little village?'

'Penfold,' Comfort murmured reading the sign. The lane had widened and there were grassy verges on either side and red-brick council houses on the outskirts of the village with washing hanging on lines and rows of cabbages and onions and dahlias. In the middle of the village was an old grey church with yew trees round it and a village green in front about the size of two tennis courts. Old cottages clustered round the green, each cottage different, whitewashed or rose-coloured brick, thatched or with a steep brown-tiled roof. Old cottages such a reasonable distance from London fetched high prices and most had been bought by retired people. Outsiders. Miss Hanker stopped by a high hedge of clipped privet and a white gate.

'Is this it?' Comfort said running a nervous finger round the neck of her yellow tee-shirt, suddenly shy. She turned round for the striped suitcase, intensely aware of the children standing on the green, children appearing from the cottages round and staring in her direction. Their eyes felt like prickles on her face. Somebody new was always an event in Penfold and there had never been anybody before like Comfort. But then Granny and Grandad were coming down the path and Granny's hair was all fluffy and white round her head like a dandelion clock.

'Comfort, dear, oh my little Comfort, did you have a good journey?' Granny said her voice all husky. 'She's my own granddaughter, Comfort,' she added as Comfort flung her arms round her. Granny was warm and lavender-scented and yet you could feel her, fragile as chicken bones underneath the soft silk. 'Mind my blouse, dear, goodness what a big strong girl you are!'

Grandad was just behind, walking a little stiffly. 'Well

I never, if our little Comfort isn't almost grown up,' he said pretending to be surprised, his eyebrows whiskery as prawns above his grey eyes. He kissed her too, his tweed jacket smelling of pipe just as it had done in Harrogate.

'So kind of you, Miss Hanker, to drive Comfort all this way,' Granny was saying. 'You will stay and have a cup of tea with us, won't you?' It was going to be all right, Miss Hanker thought, her glasses misting slightly, blood was thicker than water after all.

'I'll show you your bedroom, Comfort, shall I?' Granny said leading the way up the cottage stairs which curled round in the cottage wall like the stairs in a bus. 'One attic is your bedroom and the other, well it's a sort of playroom, so there won't be any necessity for toys left around the house.' The attic ceiling sloped like a ridge tent. 'Start as we mean to go on, eh dear?' Granny finished in the rather instructive tone she had used since Miss Hanker left.

'Thanks,' Comfort said politely. What toys, she wondered, didn't Granny even know she was much to big for toys. She was talking in a new quiet voice which she thought Granny would like. She had said the cottage was really lovely and you could tell it was hundreds of years old and Granny had seemed to like that. There was a guest towel embroidered with pink clovers just for Miss Hanker and Grandad put little round tables by everybody's chair for the cup of tea and biscuits. Outside the children were playing on the green, throwing grass and calling to each other and shouting extra loud because Comfort was there.

'What a nice room! The new curtains are really

pretty,' Comfort said glancing quickly out of the window and then fixing her eyes firmly on the pink and blue daisies. What a nice room, Margaret had said every time in a new flat. Tight lips and hard words, no baths after ten and no music on Sundays, all that came later.

'Yes, well, I'm glad you like it, dear,' Granny said rather out of breath. Really the child had a sweet disposition, biddable which was more than you could say for Margaret. 'We want you to feel at home here with us because you are our *own* granddaughter when all's said and done. There's been such a lot to think of, your schooling for instance. Such a pity you turned that scholarship down, well your grandad's not made of money, not with this inflation. But there's a boarding school at Folkestone especially for children whose parents are er . . . from abroad. Margaret said you were getting on very well at school, so that's a mercy isn't it because they'll want to see your reports.'

'Margaret went to boarding school, didn't she?' Comfort said.

'The best that money could buy,' Granny said proudly and suddenly her hyacinth blue eyes were shimmering with tears. 'Such a pretty child in her pram, such golden curls, everybody turned to look. Oh dear, don't take any notice of silly old me. What a way to behave!' she said recovering and blowing her nose. 'Handsome is as handsome does. Not that you aren't pretty in your own way,' she added seeing Comfort's face forlorn in the mirror. 'Why ever have they let your hair grow so long and those earrings, quite ridiculous at your age.' She started down the stairs. A child had to be taught, guided, especially a child like Comfort. It was almost too much at her time of life, this extra cross to bear.

'I quite like earrings,' Comfort said. 'Did Margaret have earrings at my age?'

'Margaret had everything we could possibly give her. A little Princess. Your grandad spoilt her,' Granny dabbed her nose angrily with her hanky. 'That was half the trouble.'

'What trouble?' Comfort said but Granny had gone.

Reaching up she could just touch the attic ceiling in the middle, she had never had a bedroom as small as this, she had never slept on her own before either. There was a dormer window on each side and she leaned out, patting the rough brown tiles. At the back of the cottage was a garden with a flowerbed, nasturtiums, sweet williams, phlox and lots of bees. Grandad was sitting in a deck-chair just in front of the shed with a newspaper spread on his knees, puffing blue smoke from his pipe, private and content.

'Hallo,' Comfort murmured letting the word fall gently into the warm evening but Grandad did not look up.

The other way was the front garden and the green where children were still playing round two large copper beech trees which had been planted to commemorate the end of the war and were huge and spreading now. There was a girl her own age with thick rope-coloured hair and several younger ones and, when they saw Comfort at the window, they pushed each other and giggled excitedly. Comfort was excited and shy too. Getting to know the children was the best part of coming to a new place. She had lived and played in twenty London streets but this was different, everyone at Penfold was white.

'Can I play out now?' Comfort said running down. A shriek came from the green and a handful of dried grass sailed like a bird above the hedge.

'Goodness me but you've only just got here,' Granny said coming from the kitchen with a tray of clean cutlery. Rough manners and rude words would be no good at all to a child like Comfort, Granny thought, and she didn't want her teased. The small dining-room was completely filled by a mahogany table which had come from Harrogate. Granny laid cork mats on the shining brown surface. 'I really don't see any necessity for you to go out now, dear,' she added circling the table for the second time and putting lace mats on the cork ones.

'What shall I do then?' Comfort said flatly. She could see little bits of red cotton dress and white shirt through the privet hedge.

'I'm going to show you the *correct* way to lay the table,' Granny said handing her some knives.

'But I know,' Comfort said. The silver knives and forks were cold and heavy in her hand with ears of wheat embossed on the handles. 'I laid the table since I was four and cooked the tea quite often too.' Granny would approve of things like cooking the tea surely. 'I made curry for seven people once when we lived in Railton Road and . . . .'

Outside the children darted past the gate screaming like banshees.

'All that was rather different, wasn't it?' Granny said coolly. Such absence of standards, how she disliked glimpses of Margaret's way of life. 'I'm old-fashioned, Comfort, and I like things done *correctly*. The large knife is put *outside* the small knife with the sharp edges of both knives facing inwards.' Granny corrected Comfort's knives. 'They taught us that in Brownies and I've never forgotten. Life is not just a bowl of cherries, Comfort, you have to realise that.'

'I think it was for Margaret,' Comfort said staring down at the shining silver and blue and white plates which almost concealed the mahogany now. 'I think life was just a bowl of cherries for Margaret.'

'Oh, whatever are those silly children doing?' Granny said as they clustered at the gate. 'Run along now,' she shook the teacloth in her hand. 'Just run along to your own homes, please, it's getting late.'

The children slid back from the gate and stood behind the hedge, whispering quietly. 'It's that Lettie Stamp is the ring-leader, she gets the little ones into all sorts of mischief,' Granny said closing the front door. 'Tell Grandad it's time to wash his hands for dinner.'

'Dinner-time,' Comfort said stepping out into the back garden and borrowing Granny's urgent tone. But Grandad just nodded and went on puffing quietly into the evening sunshine. In the shed was a lawn-mower and piles of flowerpots, spades and rakes hung on pegs along the wall and there was a work-bench under the window with boxes of light-green seedlings. 'That window really opens, it's like a little house, this shed,' Comfort said flicking a cobweb fussily from the window latch. Carmen had a play-house, white walls, red roof and green front door, a house of her own. 'You could live out here almost.'

'I almost do, according to your granny,' Grandad said winking and tapping his pipe out on the step. 'It's a lovesome thing is a garden, peaceful. Thought you might like a bit of garden of your own?'

'Oh yes,' said Comfort looking all round and wondering which bit. 'But I don't know how to make things grow.'

'Just let them alone, that's it mostly,' Grandad said.

'Can I have that bit?' Comfort said pointing to a small square bed behind the shed which was almost out of sight of the kitchen window.

'That bit it is,' Grandad said and he looked lovingly at the clumps of red and white flowers. 'That sweet william, that's yours too. It's July now, you can get your seeds in ready for next year.'

'Next year?' said Comfort flicking through the pile of seed packets. Would she really still be at Smithy Cottage in Penfold next year? She had written to Mante at the old address but he might not get it of course. It was a bit like a message in a bottle thrown in the sea.

'Soup's getting cold, you two slow-coaches,' Granny

called from the kitchen, the smell of oxtail filled the cottage.

'I like oxtail very much,' Comfort said spreading her napkin and making a fresh start with the quiet voice. 'Is this a packet or tinned?'

'Gracious me, what a girl you are for questions,' Granny said. 'When I was a little girl it was considered bad manners to talk about food on the table. Are those children going to hang round the cottage all evening?' She added catching sight of Lettie's red dress as it flashed past the gate.

'It's our Comfort,' Grandad said as he collected up the

soup plates and put them on the hatch. 'Bound to be a seven days wonder is our little Comfort, something a bit different in a village like this, be all right once she gets to know them.'

'I don't see any necessity for Comfort to get to know them,' Granny observed slicing corned beef very thin. 'All that awful shrieking, Comfort has better things to do with her time. Every girl should be able to cook.'

'I'd quite like to play with Lettie Stamp after that,' Comfort said quickly. 'After cooking.'

'When I was your age children didn't argue about every little thing,' Granny said.

'Sorry,' said Comfort. The knives and forks rang loud on the willow-pattern plates.

'You'll soon learn our ways I'm sure, dear,' Granny said.

Comfort put her diary on the bedroom window sill and leaned out into the twilight. It was quiet now, the smaller children had been called in for bed. Swallows dived and swooped under the cottage eaves and she could see right across the fields to where the flat green land of the Romney marshes met the pink sky but she was thinking about Carmen. My complexion is Mediterranean, Carmen said over and over, you could take me for Arab easy. But Comfort herself had never minded being black. If it was all right with Margaret who had loved and married Mante, it was all right with her. But now feeling the air cold on her head where Granny had cut, the snip-snip of the sharp little scissors pecking like a chicken, she wondered if Granny minded, perhaps she would rather have a white grandchild.

'Oxtail soup and corned beef and salad,' she wrote in her diary. 'Granny is knitting me a dark green cardigan for school.'

Something moved in the deep shadow under the beech trees, Lettie was hanging by her knees swinging gently, her skirt over her head, her hair sweeping the ground. Comfort waved and Lettie swung herself up and dropped her feet down and cupped her hands round her mouth, 'You coming out?'

'Can't,' Comfort whispered already in her nightie. Downstairs the sitting-room curtains were drawn and voices came from the television, turned low for Comfort's sake.

Lettie came across the green, quiet as a stalking cat, and up the cottage path.

'What's your name then?'

'Comfort Kwatey-Jones,' Comfort said.

'How long you stopping, then?' Lettie said.

'Could be forever,' Comfort said.

'Smashing,' Lettie grinned warm and wide in the dusk below. 'I'm the oldest girl in this village, gets you down, nothing but droopy little kids, dead boring. We can be real friends can't we?'

'Yes,' said Comfort. A voice called Lettie from the far side of the green but she didn't move.

'I'll fetch you tomorrow, take you round the village. My dad says there's been us Stamps since Norman times, we're in the Domesday book and all. I can tell you anything you want to know about this village.'

'Thanks,' said Comfort.

4

Living in Penfold you could tell the time of day just by listening, cock crow passing like a message from one farm to the next as the sky began to pale, birds twittering in the eaves, the scrape of heavy boots as farm workers set out, tractors rumbling down the lane and the Rector unlatching the churchyard gate.

Comfort wrote her diary sitting up in bed and listening to the village wake round her. 'I have been here two weeks now. Yesterday I made apple-crumble and Granny let me go to the shop for sugar.' Before the diary had been something she often forgot but now it had become a necessary task, the only way she would remember. Lettie had not been back despite her promise.

After breakfast Comfort dusted the window-sills and watched the children setting out for school. Lettie went from house to house collecting the little ones and making them hold hands like a long daisy chain as they went along the lane. 'Good morning, Mrs Williams,' they chanted, 'Good morning, Mrs Davis, lovely old morning.' Every child in the village seemed to say good morning at least twenty times, Comfort thought, fancying she heard the greetings echoing round and round in the blue dome of the sky above. Penfold wasn't at all like London.

The school was an old grey stone building beyond the church with an asphalt playground round it, incongruous in the buttercups, like a wide-brimmed hat dropped by some passing giant.

'Couldn't I go to school?' Comfort said hearing 'All Things Bright and Beautiful' in the distance and longing for the clutch of hot little hands as she joined the daisy chain. 'Just till the end of term?'

'Gracious no,' Granny said. 'What could you learn in a little school like that?'

After the excitement of her arrival a shyness came between Comfort and the rest of the children and they kept away from the cottage. And besides Comfort was busy. She learned to make apple-pie with pastry made from flour and fat instead of bought in a packet and she learned to make fruit-cake and sponge-cake too. 'Light as thistledown, this sponge, just a puff of wind and it would blow itself right away,' Grandad declared, cutting himself a second slice and Comfort smiled.

'Spoiling the child,' Granny murmured at night in the bedroom below. The spaces between the old floorboards were wide enough to drop a coin through and Comfort could hear their voices and later the reassuring whistle of Grandad's snore. There were no streetlights and the night was like a black blanket laid against the cottage windows. 'Making a silly of the child, I've seen it all before,' Granny's voice was plaintive. Spoiling was no kindness, children had to learn to do what they were told, especially a child like Comfort.

Comfort wondered about the letter sent to Mante's old address but she didn't write again. Her spirit had come from Mante but her blood had come from Margaret and Granny and Grandad after all. The dark green cardigan grew two inches every night in Granny's fingers and the cottage felt safe and cosy round her and the days had a pattern again.

Comfort had her garden but she could not wait for seeds to grow. She bought six mauve and purple pansy plants from the village shop, which sold everything from bootlaces to sliced bread, planted three in her own garden and three in Grandad's.

'Real bobby dazzlers, those pansies,' Grandad said bending down to pat the soil firm round them. It was goodness knows how many years since anybody had given him an unexpected present. The petal faces quivered just as the butterflies quivered on the buddleia bush which Grandad planted especially for them, filling the back garden with peacocks and tortoise-shells all July and August.

Sometimes Comfort and Grandad went for a walk in the afternoon. Down the lane and over the railway line and along the canal. Grandad liked to see the fish which jumped in the silvery water and occasionally a heron poised on the bank. Comfort liked to see the Watkins' little house by the railway line with its muddy garden where pigs rooted, chickens pecked and cats streaked.

'Good afternoon, Mrs Watkins,' Grandad said raising his cap a clear two inches off his head, something he did for no one else.

'Afternoon,' Mrs Watkins murmured standing in her doorway, smiling sleepily over the baby's head. Earthy smells, sour and warm, wafted from the dark room behind her.

'How many children has she got?' Comfort whispered.

'Can't say exactly,' Grandad muttered, resettling the cap back on his head. 'Don't know that she's too sure.'

'Don't they go to school?' Comfort said looking back. The Watkins children had a home-made see-saw, a plank and petrol drum, and waved their bread and jam in silent greeting.

'They do sometimes. Original stock shouldn't wonder,' Grandad said. He read a lot of history. Before the villages there were ancient settlements overrun by Romans or Danes, vigorous invaders who stayed and settled down. The Watkins could be throwbacks to the original inhabitants, nomads who grew crops until the soil was spent and then moved on. Why hadn't the Watkins moved, Comfort wondered. Lapwings called across the marshes, a melancholy sound. Comfort Kwatey-Jones you have a long way to go.

'What a good girl,' Granny said after Comfort's rice pudding that evening. She was pleased with Comfort now, sometimes she hugged her suddenly or patted her head though she was always short afterwards as if she regretted her affectionate display.

'Could I have a kitten from the Watkins?' Comfort said. 'I always wanted a kitten but we moved such a lot.'

'No kittens,' Granny said firmly. 'I've never cared for cats. You'll be at school and I've got quite enough to see to.' No good came from indulgence to children, didn't she know?

The pattern of the days changed when school broke up and the children came down the middle of the lane singing,

'No more Latin, no more French
No more sitting on a hard old bench,'

as loud as they could, waving their drawings and swinging their school bags round their head.

45

'Six weeks of dreadful racket,' Granny sighed. 'And that ridiculous song when they don't even learn French, let alone Latin.'

'Traditional,' Grandad said. 'It's what their parents sang.' The children had stopped outside the cottage and Lettie walked up the brick path and knocked on the front door.

'Can *she* come out to play?' Lettie said jerking her head towards Comfort. She carried a pile of old exercise books in her arms and her green eyes were bold in her hot pink face, ready for anything. Hadn't she just finished six years at Penfold School where Miss Slade and Mrs Arthur both had their knives into her.

'I don't really see any necessity . . . .' Granny began but catching sight of Comfort at the kitchen door with her face forlorn and her hands all floury, she relented. 'Oh, go out and play, child, but no screaming, mind.'

'Course not,' Lettie said primly and Comfort followed her down the path and across the grass which was cut short now and dried in the sun like yellow dog fur. Some twenty children were waiting under the copper beech trees and Comfort smiled carefully.

'It's *her*,' Lettie's little brother, Bobby, whispered, jigging up and down. 'She's coming out to play.'

'Who? What's she want to come out for?' Betty said sulkily. She was almost nine and working hard to be Lettie's best friend.

'The black girl. She's coming out to play with us,' Bobby hiss-whispered.

'You shut up, you,' Lettie said cuffing his head which was something she did quite often. 'Who you calling black, showing your ignorance? You want your mouth washed out with soap, you do.'

'I'm telling Mum, you wait,' Bobby gulped but he did not go. The others spread out in a circle round her, blue eyes, green eyes, grey eyes, brown eyes staring. Comfort was used to staring but these eyes seemed different, gentler, as if they had taken their colour from the sky, grass, earth and water of the marsh itself.

'Stop staring, stop being rude,' Lettie said, ashamed at the unsophisticated way that her group was behaving. 'You get them everywhere nowadays, people like her. Don't you ever watch the telly? What are we all going to play then?'

'Grandmother's footsteps,' Bobby said, wisely selecting a game in which older ones did not have all the advantage.

'Does *she* know Grandmother's footsteps?' Betty nodded towards Comfort. 'They might not have it where she comes from?'

'I come from London,' Comfort said still smiling. You always had to smile till your cheeks ached in a new place. There were rules people told you and rules you had to find out for yourself.

'I'll be Grandmother if you like?' Lettie said and nobody argued though they muttered a bit when Lettie kept turning round and shouting everybody back except Comfort. What kind of Grandmother would Comfort be, everybody wondered and Comfort wondered too, lenient or strict, sending back people if they breathed even. She had been like that in Shepherds Bush one time, Clapham, too, but it wouldn't be right when she was new in Penfold. She didn't stay Grandmother long and it was Lettie she allowed to touch her shoulder first. One or two shouted 'Not fair,' but they went on playing just the same. They left for their dinners and came back for a game of kick-the-can because Lettie ruled in Penfold, okay, and a new girl in the village was exciting.

'I'm all out of puff with these kids' games,' Lettie said dropping down in the grass.

'Me too,' Comfort said dropping beside her.

'Where do you come from then?' Betty asked looping back her hair and fastening her blue butterfly slide.

'London,' Comfort said. 'I was born in London. My mum and me always lived in London.'

'You English then?' Lettie said, her round green eyes rolled thoughtfully towards Comfort.

'Well, I'm half-English, half-Ghanaian,' Comfort said.

'Half-Ghanaian? What's that when it's at home?' Betty said raising a titter from the other children.

'Oh, buzz off, you lot,' Lettie said impatiently. 'What you want to hang round us for all the time?'

'Bossy knickers, village green don't belong to you, Lettie Stamp,' Betty said. She and the others gathered disconsolately at the edge of the green and waited, preferring Lettie's tyrannies to the dullness of playing without her.

'Let's get shot of the little kids, shall we?' Lettie said putting her arm round Comfort's shoulders and steering her across the lane and through the churchyard gate. 'You're not allowed in the churchyard,' she shouted threateningly when the others tried to follow. 'Rector'll catch you and then you'll cop it.'

'Are *we* allowed then?' Comfort said anxiously as Lettie led her round the back of the church.

'Course we are, leastways you're allowed if you're with me,' Lettie said. 'I'm in the choir, and my great-granny only died three months back, so I'm allowed in to put flowers on her grave, see, so I'm twice allowed.' Even so

Lettie felt suddenly shy, she picked a few moon-daisies from the long grass and filled a glass jar from a tap fixed to the church wall until it passed off. She had longed for a friend her own age all her life, prayed to God every night and now there was this black girl and the village agog. Lettie didn't know whether to laugh or cry.

Comfort stared up at the grey church wall blotched with green and orange lichen, there were nests of swallows under the roof. Did the swallows come back year

after year to the same place, a nest of their own, she wondered. The church was part Norman, Normans had come from France, immigrants, Grandad said. Like everything in Penfold it had stood where it was for a long time. Round white clouds like cherubs billowed across the sky and there were bright green paths mown in the feathery grass where people could walk between the graves. The church was on a slight mound and the Romney marshes stretched away like an endless green ocean. It had been under the sea at one time, Grandad said, it was man-made land drained by the Romans with hundreds of dykes criss-crossing it in straight black lines and grey roads raised on banks above the grass.

'You can sit on my great-granny's grave if you like,' Lettie said extending her arm to the marble edge in hostess style. 'Grass might be damp.'

'Thanks,' said Comfort. There was a headstone made of speckly imitation marble with *Letitia Stamp* and the date of her birth and death in gold-filled letters and lots of bright green chips like bath salts.

'Saves weeding, saves cutting the grass,' Lettie explained flattening the green chips with the palm of her hand to accommodate the jar of moon daisies. 'My great-granny went to school in a white pinny, same school,' she nodded her head towards the deserted building. 'We got this photo, *Letitia* same as me,' her eyes turned to Comfort curiously. 'Where are your great-grannies then? You got four, everybody has.'

'Well, there's one in Harrogate, I think,' Comfort said startled by the question and feeling it shameful not to know for certain but nobody had ever talked to her of great-grandmothers. There must be two in Africa. She could imagine them if she tried, *dream-see* Carmen called it, buried close to the sea, sand and little dusty plants like sea-holly and palm trees above. It would be nice to really *know* your great-grannies had been to the same school as you and were safe in the earth beneath you. That was roots. You would really belong to Penfold then.

'Did you like that school?' Comfort asked.

'Blooming awful, same teachers first to last,' Lettie said fiercely. 'I'm going to the big school next term, Dunton Wood Comprehensive, it's a fresh start my mum says.' Lettie sighed as if she didn't have much confidence in fresh starts. 'Brown blazers and yellow shirts. Are you going to Dunton Wood; be brilliant if you was going to Dunton Wood?'

Comfort shook her head. The back of the dark green cardigan was finished already, spread out on the sofa arm, knitted was warmer than shop bought and Folkestone could be bracing. 'Going to weekly boarding school in Folkestone.'

'Boarding school? Fancy a girl like you going to a boarding school?' Lettie's eyes were wide with amazement. 'All posh like Felicity Davis?'

'Who's she?' Comfort said.

'Mr and Mrs Davis are *only* the most important people in this village, that's all,' Lettie said astonished at such ignorance when Comfort had been in Penfold for at least two weeks. 'They *only* live in the Manor House and have the biggest farm on the marsh and their grandfather *only* planted the copper beeches on the green and they only have the bean-field where the whole village goes picking, that's all. Still I suppose you wouldn't know, would you, your granny being a foreigner?' Lettie added in a molllifying tone. 'Our Dad's cowman at Manor House Farm.'

51

'Foreigner?' Comfort said. 'My Granny's as English as English.'

'But she hasn't lived here long, you can't call two years long. Nearly all foreigners in the old cottages, foreigners aren't village, you can't call them village. Anyway wild horses wouldn't get me going to any blinking boarding school.' Lettie dusted the top of the headstone with the skirt of her dress. 'Still we can be brilliant friends for the holidays and weekends, can't we?'

'Okay then,' Comfort said.

'Want to see something magic? Lettie said running across to the railings. 'Woolly, Woolly,' she called into the field beyond. 'Come up, come up Woolly.' The flock of grazing sheep raised their heads uneasily and lumbered away but one large lamb trotted boldly towards Lettie's outstretched hand with its handful of long fresh grass.

'Magic, eh, my *sock* lamb?' Lettie looked back over her shoulder at Comfort's wide eyes, the balance between them restored. 'Lost his mother when he was born and now he thinks I'm his mother, see, because he slept in our kitchen and I gave him his bottle every day, didn't I, little Woolly? You can pat him if you like.' Comfort stretched her arm through the railings and patted the thick wool, springy dense and oily to the touch. Having a lamb which came when you called really did seem like magic.

'So you're one of Lettie's minions now?' Granny said teasingly a few days later but she seemed relieved.

'Children need other children to knock their corners off,' Grandad said.

Comfort just smiled. She had had lots of best friends in different places, Addie and Carmen and Mercy, but she had never had quite such a good best friend as Lettie. The two of them spent all the time they could together, sitting at the far side of the church. Lettie liked to hear about Comfort's London life, planting her heels firmly in the grass and rolling her eyes as she considered the fourteen schools and twenty-five flats. But she liked to talk even more and she knew everything there was to know about Penfold, who was cousin to whom, who didn't speak to whom and Comfort had an insatiable longing to know about the village. Knowing was roots. Listening to Lettie you could get to know everything about Penfold just as you could get to know every fish and pebble in a goldfish bowl.

'Good morning, Mr Davis,' Lettie sang out. She seemed able to tell his tractor from all the other tractors and ran to open the gate with a special smile. The Rector was next in esteem being close to God and understanding how to get supplementary benefit better than anybody else. After Rector was Jim who kept the pub, Lettie said, counting on her fingers and arranging the whole village into widening layers of importance, a shape like a Christmas tree. Right at the bottom were the Watkins who kept the gates at the level-crossing until a train crashed through because they forgot. There were no trains any more and the Watkins only came to school for their free meals, sometimes they even came without knickers.

'Can't we play with the Watkins sometimes?' Comfort asked one day as they crossed the railway line on their way back from Woodfield, the next village, and tea with Lettie's Auntie Em.

'We're not allowed,' Lettie said. 'Do you want to get nits?'

'Can't we go to church?' Comfort said to Granny one Sunday. She could hardly get through the desert of the day, with Lettie singing in the choir morning and evening and wanted at home to help with the roast and visiting aunts.

'We're not really churchy people,' Granny said pursing her lips and measuring the green cardigan sleeve against Comfort's arm. 'I don't need any church to tell me what's right, I think I do my duty.' It was her *duty* to care for Comfort, she thought, decreasing one stitch at the beginning of the row for the shoulder shaping. She would hardly have credited how fond she had grown of the child in spite of everything. Such feelings were almost a weakness at her time of life, a hostage given to fortune. Granny blew her nose vigorously and cast off one stitch at the end of the row.

'You don't go to church and you don't go bean-picking either,' Comfort said reproachfuly because bean-picking looked like being a whole fortnight of desert Sundays. You could only go bean-picking with your own family, Lettie said, not altogether certain that Comfort could go with them. It depended on her granny who was quite a tartar and didn't care for people staring.

'Bean-picking? I should think not at our time of life,' Granny said. 'Pass me that wool.'

Later that evening Comfort wandered into the churchyard. It was after evensong and the church was quiet now, the red ball of the sun turning the grass to gold. Swallows gathered on the telegraph wires in long lines. They knew the days were shorter, Grandad said, they were getting ready to go to Africa. 'Come up, Woolly, come up, Woolly,' Comfort called softly and the sock lamb detached himself from the flock and came trotting to the gate taking the grass she offered. If it was magic Comfort had it too.

'What do you think you're blooming well doing?' Lettie shouted diving across the churchyard, pink with anger. 'You're not allowed in here unless you're with me. He's my lamb, Woolly is.' What a pity Lettie wasn't as pretty as her sister Auntie Em had said with the door not quite shut.

'Course I'm allowed,' Comfort said. 'Church belongs to everybody, Lettie Stamp.'

'I'm telling Rector. You don't even go to church and your granny doesn't either and she's a foreigner in this village and goodness knows what you are,' Lettie stomped up the lane.

'Course I do, I was born in England,' Comfort said stoutly. You had to stand up for yourself, Margaret said, don't let people trample you. But Lettie was angry. Would the Rector be angry too, going turkey-pink and shouting, Comfort wondered. She hated it when people got angry. It ended things, meant damage said and done which could never be undone. Like the night in Brixton. Suddenly the sound of crashing glass and people running and a white rexine chair leaping from a shop window and along the pavement as if by its own volition. There was glass all over the pavement next day, skittering under their feet like ice as they crossed to the taxi. She had been going to leave anyway, Margaret said.

Lettie was walking more slowly now and she stopped altogether at the rectory gate and began to pick a bunch of cow parsley for her rabbit. 'Want to see something funny?' she called presently.

'What?' said Comfort relief surging through her like warm water because they were friends again.

'You want to look through the windows then,' Lettie said nodding her head towards the school and turning down the lane. Comfort walked across the empty playground and jumped as high as she could, her fingers scrabbling at the gritty sill. For a few seconds she looked into the classroom, seeing small tables and chairs stacked upside down and paintings round the wall, a black face with round black eyes and a strip of yellow tee-shirt and gold earrings. Comfort landed back on the asphalt with a thump.

'Who says I look like that?' she demanded. Lettie had disappeared. The feelings whirled and fluctuated in Comfort's head like bonfire smoke on a windy day. The paintings certainly weren't beautiful. But how could you expect beautiful paintings from young kids. She was in the heads of all the children of Penfold School forever like Lettie's great-grandmother in her white pinny. 'Seven paintings of me on the school wall,' Comfort wrote in her diary that night. 'I've been painted by Dave, Ruth, Betty, Daisy, Lettie, Jim, Joy, Carol.' Whatever happened, everybody would remember her coming to the village. Granny and Grandad would always be foreigners but Comfort herself was part of Penfold.

'You can come bean-picking with us if you like,' Lettie said coming round to the cottage early on the Monday morning just as if nothing had happened. There were people gathered outside Manor House Farm waiting already. Bean-picking was the next best thing to a holiday because relations came over from Woodfield and other villages to help and there was lots of 'How he's grown!' and 'Give your Auntie Biddy a kiss then.'

'You coming with us, Comfort?' said Granny Stamp, her head tied up in a parrot green scarf. 'Don't have too much to say for yourself then.'

'I'll show her what to do?' Lettie said as Mr Davis opened the gate. A whole field was twining bean-plants, scarlet blossom mixed with green pods. A pile of sacks lay by the gate.

'It's nice doing it together, be brilliant doing it together,' Lettie said taking two sacks and explaining how you had to get your sack weighed so as to get the right money at the end of the day. Comfort nodded, already picking, her hands darting like lizards in the green leaves quickening the pace of everybody round her.

'You got a real knack,' Mrs Stamp said smiling. She was a small, sad, dark-eyed woman.

'She's a good, quick picker, I will say that for her,' Granny Stamp said. Comfort smiled and went on picking.

'Very good for your age,' Mr Davis said, weighing her third sack. 'Ever done it before?'

'No,' said Comfort taking another sack. But she had a strange feeling that she had, dream-seeing herself picking under a blue sky with the air hot and voices of women near and far away. She saw Granny cross towards the bean-field stopping a moment to talk to Mr Davis at the gate and then coming on with something fluttering in her hand. A blue airmail letter.

'It's from your father,' she said and her voice sounded husky and her eyes were pink. 'He wants you to go to Ghana,' she said. 'At once.'

5

There was such a great juddering and shuddering as the plane roared along the runway but then it rose into the blue evening like a swan rising from a lake and though the engine still roared, the quiet of the sky seemed like silence.

Below lights were winking and blinking but she could no longer see Granny and Grandad and perhaps she would never see them again. Comfort played with the thought like a cat plays with a mouse. Was it terrible or a bit sad or not sad at all. How could she even think of being sad when she was going to live with Mante in Ghana.

Granny had been very upset when Miss Hanker came with another social worker and forms to sign, so upset it was Comfort who had to make the sponge-cake for tea in the sitting-room with the little tables, Comfort who had to put the clover-embroidered guest towel in the bathroom. 'Hush now, the child will be better off with her own father, growing up with her own people,' Grandad muttered, patting Granny's arm and Miss Hanker and her colleague murmured soothingly like doves. 'Am I not her own people?' Granny asked with her eyes wide. The question hung in the air unanswered. 'We had to inform the Ghanaian police when the accident happened,' Miss

Hanker murmured. 'That's routine, I'm only sorry it all took so long. There was this confusion about the names.' 'What confusion?' Granny said indignantly. She had never trusted social workers and she never would, noseying about in other people's business. Comfort nibbled a biscuit. She didn't know whether she was going to Ghana *because* of the letter she'd sent or because of Miss Hanker's inquiries. She hadn't told Granny about the letter, she hadn't told anybody, and now it seemed better not to. The dark green cardigan was finished and carefully pressed and sewn together but it didn't seem likely that Comfort would wear it now.

'Barley sugar?' the air hostess inquired coming round with a pile on a small tray. Her smile was shiny red and wet like a new-painted pillarbox.

'Thanks. Can I have two?' Comfort said wondering whether there would be barley sugar in Ghana. For a moment she thought lovingly of the large jars of sweets along the shelf in the shop at Penfold, the tinkling sound as they hit the brass bowl on the scales.

'As many as you like, dear,' the air hostess said, still smiling, and Comfort put one in her pocket just in case.

It was October now. Arranging the ticket and passport and forms had taken longer than anybody expected. The swallows had left Penfold long ago and the telegraph wires were bare black lines twanging bleakly in the cold wind from the sea. In the cottage gardens yellow chrysanthemums drooped rain-soaked heads and leaves lay in amber drifts along the gutters.

The children had gone back to school. Betty was *big girl* now, collecting the younger ones. Little Freddie

Bone, not five yet, had cried every day that first week which would never have happened in Lettie's time, people said. There were different paintings on the school wall, space-ships and days by the sea. Lettie had a too-big brown and yellow uniform and a new friend from Woodfield who came over for Saturday tea. Comfort and Grandad went for walks again but there were only hens and pigs in the Watkins garden; the Rector had got a clothing grant for the Watkins children, people said, it was all right for some.

All through September Comfort practised her sponge-cakes. In Ghana children were expected to help at a very young age, to *bring something home*. She had asked the lady in the mobile library to get a book about Ghana and she read all about cocoa and bougainvillaea, round thatch-ed huts and sky-scrapers and paramount chiefs who sat under double-decker parasols. But it was like a scrabbled jigsaw in her head and she had no idea what the picture would finally be. Was the new address on Mante's letter, 3, Hillside Estate, a mud hut or a sky-scraper. Besides Comfort couldn't be absolutely certain she was going with Granny *not wanting* her to go so much.

It was not until she was at Heathrow airport with people all round giving each other flowers and funny dolls that Comfort began to be certain. And when the striped suit-case was weighed in and disappeared along a moving belt, then Comfort was *quite* sure. She held tight to the red handbag which contained her passport and ticket.

'You mustn't forget us, Comfort,' Granny said. Her voice was jerky like a robot's and Comfort hoped desperately that she wasn't going to cry there in the airport. 'Promise me you'll write. Put it in your diary, dear, that nice diary Granny gave you, the day you're going to write, *Thursday*, shall we say?'

'Tut-tut,' Grandad was saying watching the flight board as if he could accelerate it with the pressing beam of his eyes. Hadn't he always hated tears, scenes, rather have a leg off any day of the week. 'Ah, you're boarding now, Comfort,' he shouted quite truimphant.

'Doesn't a grandmother have rights?' Granny said addressing the whole departure lounge, her hat askew and her mouth twitching.

'Go along then, Comfort, off you go,' Grandad said gripping Granny's arm as the other passengers funnelled through the departure door.

'Goodbye, then,' Comfort brushed a quick kiss on Grandad's chin, feeling it bristly and Granny's cheek, wet as rose petals.

'I shall never see the necessity . . . .' Granny's high thin voice followed her through the door but Comfort did not look back.

For weeks she had thought about Ghana all the time but now, looking down at the curling silver line of the Thames, all she could think of was Granny and Grandad travelling back to Charing Cross, Lettie hunched over her homework by the bedside lamp her mother had got in the market for the fresh start at the new school, darkness creeping over the marsh like black water and the distant bleat of sheep.

'Are you going to settle down now?' the air hostess said collecting the dinner tray two hours later and putting Comfort's seat back. Comfort didn't feel at all like settling down and she hadn't done her teeth but the window was a black square now with an occasional wraith of cloud. She closed her eyes and when she opened them the cabin was bright white like vanilla ice cream and the air hostess was shaking her shoulder. 'Wake up, Comfort, you're in Ghana. Accra airport.'

As Comfort emerged from the belly of the plane, Mante was standing on the balcony with his arms spread in a wide gesture of welcome and she knew him at once. He was her father and her spirit came from him. It was a picture she would remember all her life.

'Comfort,' he said as she came through customs and passport control a few minutes later. 'Comfort.' Such a deep, thick-honey sound, nobody had ever said her name like that before. Her eyes seemed to take in more than usual, every detail imprinted bright and clear at a single glance, the white of his shirt, his dark silk tie, the gold watch worn outside his shirt sleeve, the cream jacket over his arm. 'Comfort, my daughter.' He took her hand and then wrapped his arms right round, warm and smelling of aftershave and violets. 'My child.' His hand lying on her arm was the hand she remembered from the pushcart and she dipped her head and kissed it. She could feel his chest shaking as he laughed joyously, his mouth wide above her head, the line of his jaw dark brown as mahogany. 'This is so fine, such a fine beautiful day for me,' he said talking and laughing at the same time, there were tears standing in his eyes. 'Such a fine big girl you have grown, my Comfort,' he said, smiling all round as if her arrival was a treat for everybody. 'This is my daughter, Comfort, come from England.'

'Hello,' Comfort smiled carefully. All round people were pushing forward and shaking her hand, men in suits like Mante, women with long cloths wrapped round their waists and babies on their back. Everybody seemed to know everybody.

'Aye-aye, it's Mante's daughter,' they said laughing and patting her. 'Mante Kwatey-Jones has a *been-to* daughter.'

It didn't seem quite right to Comfort when she hadn't so much been-to England as come-from. Mante steered her out of the airport building, towards the hotel opposite. He walked as if he had springs in his feet, a bouncing walk, a party walk, and Comfort tried to walk the same way. The concrete airfield shimmered in the heat like a pan of boiling milk and there was a faint sound of drumming in the air which seemed to come from no particular direction but just to be part of the hot blue air. There was a shaded balcony with table and chairs and cascading sprays of brilliant magenta blooms.

'Bougainvillaea?' Comfort said pleased to find at least one thing she knew. She wanted to tell Mante how much she had wanted to come but it was difficult with people calling out from the pavement and the noise of the airplane seemed trapped inside her head as the sound of the sea is trapped inside a shell.

'Coca-cola for two here,' Mante said smiling expansivly. And Comfort smiled too, letting the careful smile she had worn in England spread into a great wide smile that relaxed her cheeks and parted her lips, smiling the way everybody seemed to smile here.

'Aye-aye, it's the child from England,' people said, waving mauve-palmed hands from the pavement or running up the steps to clap Mante's shoulder.

'Are they *all* your friends?' Comfort asked.

'All,' said Mante. 'They are Ga people, people of my tribe and yours, a big family.'

'Ga?' said Comfort softly. 'I am Ga?' She hadn't thought of herself as belonging to a tribe.

'Now let me really look at you,' Mante said. His voice was like sea rumbling in a cave, Comfort thought; surely she could remember the rumble of his voice in the Lewisham flat. 'My big daughter who writes to me and wants to come to live in Ghana.'

'You got my letter then?' Comfort said. So it was *she* who had fixed it and not Miss Hanker.

'Of course I got your letter,' Mante said. 'But why did you send it to the old address?'

'I hadn't got your new address,' Comfort said. There was so much to explain. She wanted to take his hand, look at his heart-line and life-line, Mrs Mace had shown her how to tell fortunes, but Mante seemed to need his hand for waving as he talked.

'Margaret had it surely?'

'She didn't keep letters much,' Comfort said. 'It must have got lost when we moved.'

'Lost, lost,' Mante sighed and seemed to sink into a moment of sadness. 'You saw the accident, child?'

'Yes, it was a bus, she saw somebody and ran across the road,' Comfort said flatly. She had had to say it quite often but it was something she tried not to think about. She had pinned that week of her diary together with a paper clip.

'She had so many friends, it was her nature to have friends,' Mante said speaking to Comfort and to the people at the next table too. It seemed it was the right thing here to share your private thoughts. 'My wife, Margaret, killed by a bus, the mother of this child. Such a loving and giving woman, Saturday's child, isn't it?'

'Sorry, sorry,' the woman at the next table said nodding her head rhythmically. 'But the child will bring solace, such a pretty pale-skinned child like Jerry Rawlings, him they call Junior Jesus. Sorry, sorry.'

'Your grandmother took good care of you?' Mante asked.

'Oh yes, Granny wanted me to stay with them and go to this school in Folkestone,' Comfort said and hesitated. 'But a child's spirit comes from her father.'

'Aye-aye, the child knows the Ghanaian way of thinking already,' the woman clapped her hands.

'She is a Ghanaian girl,' Mante said proudly. The woman left a few minutes later and he leaned back in his chair and talked more quietly. He didn't seem in any hurry to leave. 'Efua is your mother now. Efua is a very beautiful woman, indeed she was beauty queen in her own town five years ago, Miss Axim.'

'Should I call her *Mother*?' Comfort said.

'Of course,' Mante said. 'Just as you call me *Father*. But Efua is a modern woman, an air hostess until she had to stop because of the baby expected soon.' Mante smiled tenderly. He had been waiting for this baby for a long time, praying to the Christian God and Onyame as well. Now at last the baby was coming but it was a difficult time, a mixed-up time, the best gynaecologist money could buy and Efua talking of ghosts like any village woman. 'Efua has not been well these past months. You must try and not cause any trouble, Comfort. Later you can help with the baby.'

'When I'm not at school,' Comfort said.

'Hear what I am telling you, Comfort,' Mante said firmly. 'Such difficult times, inflation rising and rising and nothing in the shops, it isn't good for Efua to get angry, it isn't good for the baby. She is not a strong woman. Your grandmother now, she is a strong woman, very strong.'

'Granny at Penfold?' Comfort said.

'You are in Ghana now. I speak of your grandmother in Wanwangeri where things are better because they grow their own food. A very strong woman with her own farms and her own lorry and a mind of her own too,' Mante smiled ruefully. 'A strong-strong mind that sent me to live at the mission school at five years old until I got a scholarshop to Achimota School. Now I work in the civil service, now I am a 'fridgeful', 'carful' man, all because of my mother's strong mind. Your grandmother wants to see you very much, Wanwangeri is about seventy kilometres.'

'I want to see her too,' said Comfort politely. 'Perhaps I could go in the holidays? When am I starting school?' Not that she wanted to start exactly because being away from school for so long she would have forgotten such a lot.

'Soon,' said Mante but there was a certain vagueness in his voice. The balcony was empty now and his expression had become serious. Had she said something to annoy him, Comfort wondered. 'We will go to the house now and I will show you Achimota School on the way.'

It had been getting steadily hotter and the side of Mante's car was like a boiling kettle. He had to spread a rug across the seat before they could get in. It was cooler once they were moving, driving along a grey road raised on steep banks above the Accra plain which stretched away to the line of palms along the coast. The earth was red, hard-baked and dry like a terracotta flowerpot and thinly covered with grass which shimmered green in the distance but disappeared as you got close, a blade here and there like hairs on a bald red scalp. There were thorn bushes too and animals grazing where they could, gaunt fawn cows with wide spreading horns which stood from their head like the handlebars of bicycles. A small boy tending them, raised his arm and waved, teeth flashing as Mante waved back and Comfort waved too. Everyone greeted everyone here, she thought, as if they were all part of the same family.

'Achimota School,' Mante whispered, his voice curiously intense as they drove in the gates and up the driveway under an avenue of trees. White buildings with graceful rounded doorways and steep roofs. 'The best years of your life, don't they say?' He was smiling as they circled a bed of scarlet canna lilies at the top of the drive, visiting his boyhood. 'They were good years for me. Achimota, the word means *do not mention the name*, something to do with slavery, they say. This place was the last chance of escape before the slaves were shipped across the sea. The world was spoilt then.' Comfort stared at a patch of yellow green bamboo, a place to hide, had it been there then, she wondered.

'Achimota,' she murmured a rushy, whispering sound like wind in leaves. A teacher's voice came sharp and clear from a nearby classroom, several heads looked up from desks to gaze in their direction.

'Now Achimota is just a school,' Mante went on dreamily. 'Built on high principles, loyalty to tribe. Eton, you have heard of the playing fields of Eton where the English won their battles? See that lamp-post, it is a memorial to a boy who died running for his house, his heart couldn't stand the strain. It was a long time ago, long before my time, things are different here now. Everything changes.'

'Will I be going to this school?' Comfort said.

'We shall have to see,' her father said smiling. 'It is hard to get in, there's an entrance examination.'

'I'm quite good at exams,' Comfort said diffidently. 'At least I used to be. Margaret said I might train to be a doctor.'

'It is not just the exam,' Mante said. 'Important people want to send their children here, nowadays it is all *dash*. The dash is a present which helps things along.'

'Like a sort of bribe?' Comfort said.

'Be careful what you say, Comfort,' Mante said changing gear abruptly and moving on. 'It is easy to offend people with bad manners and talk of bribes. Girls your age are not expected to give their opinion all the time in Ghana.'

'Sorry,' Comfort murmured. 'Sorry.'

'You will soon learn our ways, Ghanaian ways,' her father said forgivingly. They had turned onto the unmade road of Hillside Estate. Red dust, *swish*, rose in a cloud round them and covered the white bonnet of the car like pollen. There were bungalows on each side with orange and grapefruit trees between them. 'This is my house.' It was built round a small patio garden with banana trees and grass. There was a veranda all round with rooms leading off. 'Efua?' he called and Comfort smiled the careful smile. A middle-aged man in khaki shorts appeared at the kitchen door smiling and nodding. 'This is John, my steward,' Mante said putting his hand on John's shoulder. 'Very good steward.'

'Master's pikkin go come from England?' John said nodding towards Comfort, his smile showing broken teeth. Fancy having servants, Comfort thought, it was like the telly, '*Upstairs, Downstairs.*' 'Nice pikkin, fine-fine pikkin. Missus say hot-hot day, she go bedroom.' Mosquito screens like brown chiffon covered the veranda at the bedroom side.

'Welcome, Comfort, welcome daughter,' Efua said coming from behind it. She was tall and wearing a blue housecoat which belled out like a tent in front of her. Her hair was cut very short to go under the fashionable wig she wore to go out and her eyes were wide-spaced, beautiful red-brown eyes with thick curling lashes. But though she was smiling now at Comfort, there was something dissatisfied about the set of her mouth. 'So this is your daughter, Mante?' she said taking Comfort's hand and turning her slowly round. 'She is not much like her father I am thinking but a child is always a blessing. Why was your father choosing an old fashioned name like Comfort?' she added teasingly.

'She was called after my mother as my first daughter,' Mante said tersely. 'It is the custom in our family as you know.'

'It's nice to be here anyway,' Comfort said in the awkward pause that followed. 'I'm glad to be with my father and mother.'

'Aye-aye, the child has good manners at least,' Efua said. 'We hear bad things of children in England. A child without respect is ashes in the mouth of his parents. Come, I will show you where you are going to sleep.'

The bedroom was square and airy with two beds, a chest of drawers against the wall and a white dropside cot gleamingly new standing in the middle. The curtains had a bear with boots and a black hat.

'Paddington,' Comfort said, her eyes widening with surprise. 'Fancy finding Paddington Bear curtains in Ghana.'

'You like them?' Efua said smiling. 'A friend got them

for me in England. You cannot get modern stuff here any more. In Accra market you can buy anything from okra to a corpse's fingers, that's what they used to say but now it is all old-fangled stuff. You can sleep here with the baby, unless you have a cough,' she added. She had been married three years and humiliated and pitied for her childless state.

'I only get coughs in England,' Comfort said clicking open her case.

The table was already laid for lunch at one end of the wide living room, plates knives and forks just like England, Comfort thought, except the knives were not pointing the *correct* way. John brought tinned ham and lettuce and a dish of potatoes.

'I like water cold-cold,' Efua said testing the jug fretfully as she sat down. She spoke English well but both she and Mante talked to the steward in the pidjin English he used. 'How many times must I tell you, jug go fridge in morning?'

'Him go fridge long-long time,' John muttered, his jaw set stubbornly as he put potatoes on the table. 'But him no go cold-cold.'

'Bush-boy, what for you cross-talk me,' Efua's eyes flashed angry as John retreated to the kitchen on his bare feet. Comfort's heart was pounding unpleasantly as she cut her ham. How could she eat when Efua got so angry about such a small thing as *very* cold water? Awful things happened when people got angry.

'Eat up, Comfort,' Mante said gently. 'I expect everything here in Ghana will seem strange at first?'

'Well, it is a bit hot,' Comfort said. Beyond the shade of the veranda the light was yellow as custard and she could still hear drumming. 'But some things are the same, I mean this table with ham and lettuce and knives and forks. . .'

'Did you think we eat with our fingers?' Efua said glancing half-teasing at Mante. 'When we have important visitors, big-big people from the government, then we must show respect for African ways and eat with our fingers. Aye-aye it is too hot to eat.'

'Come, come, you must eat, Efua,' Mante pleaded. 'Think of the child, how will we have a fine son if you do not eat?'

'It is rest I need,' she said getting up abruptly. 'If we had air-conditioning I could rest . . . . all our neighbours are having air-conditioning but poor-poor Mante Kwatey-Jones cannot afford because his sisters have twenty children.'

'She will feel better when it is cooler,' her father said as Efua disappeared along the veranda. 'And you must be tired too, Comfort, everybody here lies down in the hot afternoon except poor civil servants who have to work like me,' he added with a smile. 'In the evening I work late as a taxi-driver. Nobody can live on one salary any more, so I'll see you tomorrow.'

'Goodbye then,' Comfort said. The bedroom shutters had been closed against the sun. Comfort pushed one gingerly and the hot air rushed at her face like an oven door. There was a small bowl of red-coloured palm oil on the window sill. There was no sound from the room next door, perhaps Efua had gone to sleep. Paddington Bear billowed gently against the shutters. Comfort put a ring round Thursday for the day she would write to Granny. Then she lay down and closed her eyes. She was in Ghana now where she had wanted to be.

Far away the drums beat on through the hot afternoon.

6

'I have sent for the dressmaker,' Efua said a few days later. 'There is nothing in the shops nowadays.' Comfort's cotton skirt and tee-shirt were too hot for Ghana and the message to the dressmaker was sent by word of mouth. Despite her threatening irritability on the first day, Efua had been kind to Comfort, calling her into the bedroom to see her clothes and wigs and asking her opinion about the latest styles in England. But neither Margaret nor anybody in Penfold had considered fashion important and Comfort did not have much to tell. And though she wanted to please Efua, Comfort was always glad to escape from her stepmother's troubled eyes and the questions which were never spoken. At first it had seemed to Comfort that nothing was private, that everything could be said out loud, but gradually she realised that what was private in Ghana was just different.

'Dressmaker she go come,' John said padding down the veranda on his bare feet one hot afternoon. Comfort jumped up, glad of the diversion. Efua had been out since the morning, an appointment at the hospital, she said, and the house was so quiet. Comfort had been trying to write a letter to Granny but it was particularly difficult in the heat of the afternoon. 'I am probably going to Achimota School soon,' she had written, 'Which is one of the oldest and best schools in the country. The school badge has black and white notes like a piano, ebony and ivory and . . . .' But Comfort paused because she wondered if the visit to Achimota had been more on Mante's account than hers. With his two jobs there was very little opportunity to talk and somehow she sensed that he did not want to talk about her schooling. It was as if she was a visitor at Hillside Estate, just as the swallows had been visitors at Penfold.

'Dressmaker, she go make fine-fine dress for you,' John added smiling sideways as Comfort followed him back to the kitchen. 'Where your shoes, Master say pikkin wear shoes.'

'Oh, I'll get them in a minute,' Comfort said. Going barefoot you could get hookworm, Mante had said.

The dressmaker stood at the back door. Her blue and white leopard-pattern cloth looked black and white in the bright sunlight but when she saw Comfort she smiled and stepped into the shade of the kitchen, swinging the sewing-machine down from her head onto the kitchen table. It was only then that Comfort noticed the baby tied in the cloth on her back. His small head flopped like a tulip, tiny black hairs just sprouting from the mauve scalp. He slept on as his mother slid him gently onto a cloth bed she had made under the kitchen table.

'Fine-fine baby,' Comfort said knowing by now that this was the least expected.

'Fine-fine pikkin, four boys at home,' the dressmaker said proudly, holding up five fingers so there should be no mistake. 'All fine-fine pikkin. Make fine dress for you,' she added letting the bolt of yellowish cloth, the colour of sand, unwind to the floor.

'Have you got any other stuff?' Comfort asked, used to choosing.

75

'You no like?' the dressmaker looked up from her knees on the floor with the scissors ready in her hand. 'You want green?' Her expression made it clear what she thought of green but she jerked her head towards the bolt of applegreen cloth.

'This one nice,' said John standing at the kitchen door.

'I'd like a cloth like yours,' Comfort said. 'African cloth.'

'Missus no want, Missus no like African cloth,' the dressmaker said firmly as the scissors snipped into the yellow. 'This cloth good for school.'

'School?' Comfort murmured gazing at the dressmaker as if she might have some clue but the dressmaker said nothing further.

Now she had a reason for being there Comfort stayed in the kitchen all afternoon. She had wanted to before but had been too shy. If the bungalow was oppressively silent there was usually laughter and chatter in the servant's yard. But it was quiet now in the heat of the day when everybody sat or lay in such shade as they could find. The only sound was the distant drumming like a heart beat in the hot air.

'Fine-fine dress she go make,' John murmured standing at the kitchen door cleaning his teeth with a frayed stick. The dressmaker had cut two dresses with a paper pattern, the scissors sliding through the cloth with reckless and cheerful confidence. Now the machine handle whirred in her hand.

'I hope so,' said Comfort. John was not *carful* or *air-conditionful*, not even *bicycleful* but there was an air of contentment about him, he was pleased with himself and the world. There was always somebody in the yard, people who came for a drink of water, friends from his

76

own village looking for work who often stayed for days in the tiny cramped room where John lived with his young wife, Winnie, and small son. Whoever stayed was welcomed and given the best food. 'Share meal with friend, rich in fortune,' John said. Now Winnie sat in the shaded doorway of her room while a friend did her hair into tiny plaits which stood up like kitten tails all over her head.

'Fine-fine dress,' she murmured coming to the kitchen door when her hair was done. She knew very little English but she stood talking to the dressmaker in Ga for a few minutes. She did not seem very much older than Comfort herself.

'What is she saying?' Comfort murmured looking from one to the other and burning to understand. 'Dressmaker, she say good you go come,' John said. 'She say new pikkin good for Master and Missus.'

'Have you got pikkins, John?' Comfort asked politely.

'Six pikkin,' John smiled widely. 'One here,' he jerked his head across the yard where his small son slept. 'Five in North with first wife. Me Ayambilli,' he tapped his chest with his finger and seemed to assume a new dignity with his old name. 'Ayambilli, my name in North but I go come for working here and man in office say Ayambilli no good name. He say John good name for me.'

'Shall I call you Ayambilli then?' Comfort said resenting this arbitrary change more than John seemed to himself.

'No, no,' John shook his head. 'John good name for work, Ayambilli good name for North.' He drifted away with his cleaning stick in his hand.

It was early evening when the second dress was finished and the dressmaker gathered up her bolts of cloth and tied the baby onto her back. Comfort slid the

yellow dress over her head. She liked the colour by this time and as the dressmaker had suggested it was the colour all the school girls here seemed to wear. Now she would look just like everybody else. The dress had a straight bodice cut wide and cool round the neck and arms and a flared skirt.

'Nice,' said Winnie smiling across the yard as Comfort spun round to show the back and the skirt flew out. Perhaps she and Winnie could be friends, Comfort thought, but Winnie was already preparing fufu for her family's evening meal, the long pole in her hand pounding sweet potato in the wooden bowl on the ground. Big Man, her little son, who was eighteen months and just

walking, put his thumb in his mouth and stared at
Comfort. There were beads round his neck and waist to
ward off evil. Then Comfort heard the car slide into the
garage, Efua was back calling for tea and the leisurely
pace of the yard quickened.

'Coming Missus,' John called back pulling on his
uniform shirt. Comfort followed the tea tray to the back
veranda where Efua had flopped into a wicker chair and
lay with her eyes closed.

'The dressmaker came,' Comfort said quietly. 'Do you
like my dress?' Efua's eyes clicked open. For a second she
stared at Comfort as if she didn't know who she was.

'Come here,' she said at length. 'That shoulder isn't
right.' She tweaked the offending shoulder. 'That fool
woman. This shoulder sticks right up like a wigwam.'

'It doesn't matter,' Comfort said fidgetting free. 'It's
all right, she's been working on it all afternoon.'

'How dare you cross-talk me?' Efua flared. 'You have
too-too much to say for a girl your age.'

'Sorry,' said Comfort instantly contrite. Hadn't her
father said it was bad for Efua to get upset. 'Sorry, sorry,
sorry.'

Across the thin grass she could still see the dressmaker far away, a slight, blue and white figure with the dark patch of the baby's head against her back and the sewing machine balanced on her head.

'Which day did Margaret die?' Efua asked suddenly, her tone had softened but Comfort was startled by the question and the curious brightness of Efua's eyes. Her stepmother had never mentioned Margaret before.

'June 15th,' Comfort said flatly.

'June 15th,' Efua murmured sinking back. 'And I think I have been ill since June 15th.'

'But . . . .' Comfort began. She wanted to say the two events were not connected but there was something about Efua's expression which stopped her. 'But . . . . it was a long time ago.'

'A long time,' Efua said rocking gently back and forth as she sipped her tea. 'And I have been sick-sick for a long time too.'

Comfort sat up in bed and reached for her diary. The shutters were folded back and early morning sunlight streamed through the windows making Paddington Bear's coat bright as forget-me-nots though the sky outside looked pale, slightly misty, and the air was cool. Bicycle bells tinkled as the stewards came to work from the shanty village two miles away, ringing their bells partly in farewell to their friends as they left the road and partly in celebration. It was good to be alive and very good to own a bicycle. There were better things for sure like a car, a *carful* man was much esteemed especially by women looking for a husband, but it was still good to own a bicycle.

Comfort knew the morning sounds just as she had in Penfold. She was used to bougainvillaea round the window, and the clumps of bamboo and hibiscus beyond where glossy starlings squabbled, their plumage shot turquoise-black like tiny peacocks. 'Winnie made three cedis and thirty pesawas,' Comfort wrote in her diary. Pesawas were a hundred to one cedi and a cedi had been about three to the pound, when she first arrived, but it changed all the time. How many cedis to the pound didn't matter much to Comfort and wouldn't have mattered at all except for the English money still inside the handbag.

'I have been here for a month. Winnie is my best friend now. She is teaching me the Ga tongue and has promised to take me to the shanty village. Soon I shall have a brother or sister.' Comfort sighed and bit her pencil. She had certainly expected to go the school. If she couldn't go to Achimota could she go to the nearby school, she had asked. Every day boys and girls went streaming down the road with their school books on their heads. Questions, questions, Efua said, irritably, in Ghana girls her age did not ask questions all the time. And Comfort had stopped asking. Her father did not scold her but Comfort hated to see the bafflement in his eyes as he looked in her direction, she tried not to hear the frequent arguments about money and air-conditioning and his sister's children in Wanwangeri and inflation and all the things you could not buy in Ghana any more.

Comfort still wrote in her diary every day. There was still more than a year of diary. Letters came from Granny in Penfold every week, one with a P.S. added by Grandad said the pansies were still blooming. Why hadn't she written? Granny asked, she was worried naturally, she did hope Comfort was settled at her new school and being a good girl, Lettie sent her love and seemed to expect a postcard too. Comfort sighed. Every Thursday Granny had said, but she found it difficult to read Granny's letter and almost impossible to write back. It was all so far away, it had nothing to do with her now she was a Ghanaian girl.

She must write to her granny in England, Mante said sternly one evening. Young people must show respect for older people, especially older people who had looked after them. If he was vague about her schooling he was adamant about that. And Comfort had promised. Sometimes she had done what Margaret had said and sometimes not, but she always did what Mante said because he was her father and they had the same spirit and she wanted to please him more than anything.

The late evening when he got home was the best part of the day. Efua went to bed early and Comfort sat on a wooden stool close to her father's chair. The darkness was full of sound, cicadas ticked and termites fluttered against the light. He taught her words in Ga, polite greetings, how she should address her grandmother or the headman of the village or chief.

He told her about the old Ghana which had existed in the south of the Sudan between the fourth and sixteenth centuries, a civilised kingdom at a time when the English still lived in caves and painted themselves with woad, Mante said. Later the Ga people had pushed their way across the African continent to settle along the west coast and had stayed there ever since. There had been much fighting in the old days and many killed, 'As dear and rare as youth in ancient times,' was a common saying.

Comfort stared out at the palm tree tops which looked like great black spiders against the starry sky. Everything changed, nothing stayed the same, people and birds ran round the earth's surface fluid as water. 'Shall I tell you what Margaret said?' Comfort offered. Margaret had said that different skins were adapted to different climates but now everybody moved about such adaptation did not matter anymore. In the future everybody would probably be pale brown like Comfort Margaret said, but all that would take a long time, dinosaur time. But Mante shook his head, not caring for such speculation, it was the past which interested him. Old Ghana had perished because there was no writing, Mante said. Everything was lost. He was writing a book, a history of the Ga people when he could find the time. He managed a page most evenings, black words on white paper.

Comfort promised Mante to write to Granny but sitting up in bed with the pad upon her knees she wondered what to say. The yellow dresses were no longer news and how could she say she didn't go to school when she knew Granny would have a fit and it wasn't polite in Ghana to make older people angry. She didn't think Granny would want to hear about the baby much either. Comfort sighed and stared at the layer of pink dust which lay along the top of the cot. Already she could hear the sweep of John's broom along the veranda and the rhythmic clock as it hit the wall. The previous night termites had swarmed, thousands flying against the lampshade like tiny dragonflies. Their discarded wings made a huge pile, a dry brittle sound as John swept, like glass on the pavements of Brixton, it suggested change. Comfort dressed quickly.

'Plenty-plenty termites,' John remarked gathering

wings into the dustpan. Comfort followed him along the veranda. She spent as much time as she could in the servant's quarters now. Big Man was screaming lustily in the yard as Comfort stepped out of the kitchen door and into the bright sunlight. He was covered all over now with thickly lathered white soap. Winnie seemed quite unperturbed by his screams as she scooped cold water from the bucket and poured it over him, the white suds slid down leaving his skin wet and shining as brand new wellingtons. Big Man screamed louder than ever.

'Doesn't he like being washed?' she asked in Ga.

'The water is cold,' Winnie said shrugging her plump shoulders placidly and pouring more cold water. She wore a single length of blue cloth folded round her body under her armpits. She was only sixteen herself and very proud of Big Man, especially proud, holding her head high, in a household where the Missus had been married three years and no child born yet.

Every day when Winnie had finished bathing and feeding her small son, she went out to trade, carrying the tray of sweets on her head till they reached the corner where the school children went past. And Comfort went with her. At first her stepmother had objected, it hadn't seemed quite right for a girl from England to sit at the roadside but after the first week she no longer tried to detain Comfort so long as she wore her sandals. In such difficult times it was only right that each child learned to bring something home.

So Winnie and Comfort sold sweets. Sometimes Comfort played with Big Man and sometimes she minded the tray for Winnie and took one or two pesewas from children as they passed while Winnie talked to a friend. 'You want to buy sweets?' Comfort called in English and

Ga. Winnie liked to talk more than anything and Comfort was soon fluent in Ga. Winnie talked of things her father never mentioned, charms and fetish priests and how Efua had asked her to get red palm-oil in the market to protect her from ghosts. Sensible people didn't believe in ghosts, Comfort thought. If the bowl of red palm-oil on her window sill was empty in the morning, it was because the cats drank it. But Winnie believed it was ghosts that lapped in the night and her eyes were round with fear. And as the days passed Comfort's own certainty ebbed away.

'Are you going to the Indian today?' Comfort asked as Big Man's screams subsided into hiccoughing sobs. For two weeks now she had asked the question every morning. The Indian trader lived in the shanty village and supplied Winnie with the sweets. Comfort wanted to go to the shanty village. She had hardly seen anything outside the immediate vicinity of the bungalow. But Winnie who was generous and friendly in most ways seemed reluctant to take her.

'Maybe,' Winnie said rubbing Big Man with a towel. The little boy stared mistrustfully at Comfort, full of hurt at this twice daily outrage of his cold bath.

'Can I come with you?' Comfort said. 'Please take me.'

'Why would a been-to girl from England want to go to the shanty village?' Winnie teased, hanging the wet towel on the line and loosening and then re-twisting the cloth round her body.

'I want to see it, that's all,' Comfort mumbled writing in the pink dust with her toe with the water spilled from Big Man's bath. 'I haven't been anywhere yet except the airport and Achimota school.' But it wasn't just that. The drumming which went on night and day came from the shanty village and seemed to call her like a genie from the darkness. If only she could understand its message.

'Well, I might go there today,' Winnie said with a sideways glance. 'Your stepmother has asked me to get more palm-oil for her. Aye-aye the ghosts in Hillside Estate get greedy.'

It was an hour's walk to the shanty village, a collection of huts which straggled in a half circle close to the main road. The drumming was quiet that afternoon and there was nothing magic about the shanty village itself. There was a tap and a slab of concrete in the centre where several girls waited in line to fill their buckets. All round there were windowless huts made of corrugated iron and bits of wood gleaned by pulling the nails from boxes, printed with NESTLES, FORD and SINGER which described the items the boxes had contained. Children and chickens ran everywhere and everybody seemed to know Winnie, calling out and waving as Comfort followed her to the Indian's hut which was bigger and more solidly built than the rest. Inside it was piled up with boxes of groceries from floor to ceiling, the Indian ran a shop himself as well as supplying other traders. He was a small thin man in a white, high-necked shirt and he glanced curiously at Comfort as Winnie bought her supplies but spoke too fast for her to understand.

'What did he say?' Comfort asked. For weeks she had wanted to get to the shanty village but already she was eager to get back to Hillside Estate.

'He says maybe you will start trading yourself and spoil my business,' Winnie said with a laugh as Comfort tied Big Man onto her own back with Winnie's cloth for the walk home.

'Of course I wouldn't, I promise I wouldn't,' Comfort said indignantly. 'Anyway how could I?'

'Maybe I will give you a cedi a week for wages,' Winnie said, swinging the box of sweets and the bottle of palm-oil onto her head. 'But perhaps you are going to Wanwangeri soon?'

'Wanwangeri? Why?' Comfort said.

'Your stepmother is frightened,' Winnie explained. 'She thinks it is the ghost of a jealous first wife with no son who has sent her such trouble, such sickness.'

'But it isn't, how could it be?' Comfort said.

'Why else should the Missus get sick and worse since you came?' Winnie said extending her fingers like two star-fish as she spoke. 'With Big Man I was never sick because Mr John's first wife has three sons already and cannot be jealous,' she added concluding her case. She considered it proven.

It was late when they got back to the bungalow but that evening the car was already in the garage and Comfort could hear voices on the veranda as she ran in.

'Winnie paid me a cedi as wages,' she said quickly expecting to be scolded for being out so late. But as well as her father and Efua there was another woman on the veranda, a plump-shouldered woman in a vivid black and orange cloth.

'This is your Aunt Ata, my sister,' her father said. 'What do you say to your aunt, Comfort?'

'Greetings and welcome, Aunt Ata,' said Comfort. 'I hope your trade prospers and that my grandmother is in good health?'

'The girl knows our ways already,' said Aunt Ata pleased. 'Your grandmother sends you this amulet to keep you well and safe.' She handed Comfort a tiny leather envelope on a leather thong. Inside was a white shell.

'Please thank her for me,' Comfort said putting it round her neck.

'You can thank her yourself,' Mante said softly. 'Your grandmother asks for you, Comfort. It would not be right to disappoint her, my mother to whom I owe everything.' There was a heavy sadness in his voice now. 'Everything is family here,' Mante sighed.

'The tree which stands alone is soon blown down by the storm,' Comfort recited politely. Efua's tawny eyes were fixed upon her and the veranda seemed to shift slightly and the drumming which had been quiet all afternoon started up in the darkness faraway. 'But the tree in the forest is kept safe by the others.'

'Aye-aye, you speak well,' said Aunt Ata and the rumble of her voice was like Mante's though not so deep.

'A child is better off in a village where food is grown,' Efua observed. 'Yams and cassava and plenty of fish.'

'Shall I go and pack?' Comfort said.

7

'Wake-up, Comfort, time to go for the tro-tro bus.' Aunt Ata had slept in the second bed and already she was gathering her belongings into a bundle. Outside it was still quite dark. Comfort, still muzzy with sleep, sat up and pulled her yellow dress over her head. She had got used to this bedroom but now the Paddington bear curtains and the white cot seemed like a stage set ready for her departure into the black back-drop of the African night. She had got herself to Ghana and Hillside Estate with her letter but now some other force had taken charge and was moving her on.

Comfort Kwatey-Jones, you have a long way to go.

'Come,' whispered Ata opening the door. There was no sound from the other bedroom. Her father and stepmother had said goodbye last night on the veranda. 'Be good to your grandmother and show respect,' Mante had said sadly. 'A child belongs to her family and they belong to her.'

'Yes,' Comfort said. She had felt excited then, hadn't she and Margaret always felt this excitement when they left for a new place, floating like flotsam on a river. Now she would find out what lay on the other side of the hills on the skyline. Besides she was not sorry to leave the troubled atmosphere of the bungalow, the saucers of palm-oil on her bedroom window sill and Efua's anxious carnelian gaze.

Ata's sandals shuffled along the veranda and Comfort picked up her striped case and followed. The horizon was streaked with pale yellow light where the sun would soon rise. A layer of white mist lay above the ground and the tops of the citrus trees floated like black wreckage on a white sea. The darkness was full of sounds, insects ticked in the grass, a late owl screeched.

Comfort looked back. In the grey dawn the bungalows were like squares of chocolate scattered at random across the hillside. She was no longer quite sure which one was Mante's. Her arm ached from her case and she swung it up onto her head. In the yellow school dress with the amulet round her neck she was going to Wanwangeri to see her grandmother like any Ghanaian girl. She didn't know when she would be back. 'Soon, soon,' Mante had muttered but his eyes had slid away and *soon* was a wishy-washy word that Comfort had never cared for.

'Your bag is hard-hard,' Ata said stopping to twist a

bit of cloth into a circle as a pad for Comfort's head and then walking on again. Ata laughed a great deal and moved gracefully, holding her head high to balance her bundle. The blue and yellow of her cloth became slowly visible as the sun came up. Comfort tried to walk in the same way, keeping her back straight but she still had to keep one hand on the case. Perhaps people would take them for mother and daughter, she thought, she had tried to be like Efua but Ata was her aunt after all and they had the same spirit. Ata walked as if the world belonged to her, as if despite her lack of education she understood it better and was more truly at home in it than her clever been-to brother. And Comfort wanted to walk like Ata.

The bus stop was close to where Comfort had so often sold sweets and presently the tro-tro minibus came down the road, two yellow eyes and a great deal of hooting. Ata paid three pesawas each, all the fares were three or multiples of three pesewas.

'Do we get a bus right to Wanwangeri?' Comfort said as they drove down the road.

'We go to the lorry park and get a mammy-lorry. Maybe we get there today, maybe tomorrow if the lorry breaks down,' Ata said shrugging her shoulders as if this uncertainty was an inevitable and even a pleasurable part of travelling and nothing to worry about since there was always a cousin or friend who would give you a sleeping mat for the night. Comfort gazed out of the window, the bungalows had disappeared, everything she had ever known seemed to be disappearing. She clutched her case tight.

As they reached the outskirts of Accra there were tall buildings, offices and flats on either side of the road and tucked between them a jumble of huts where hundreds of people lived, emerging now to wash at the street tap. Pressure lamps hung in doorways like large yellow pears.

'This is the stopping place,' Ata said speaking to Comfort in Ga. The lorry park was already full of mammy-lorries, Bedford vans, painted in bright and easily recognisable colours, red and blue, green and yellow. Each one had a motto painted on the bonnet, 'Sea Never Dry,' 'Poor No Friend,' 'The Lord is my Shepherd'. Early travellers had gathered already, there were no timetables just *book-men*, touting for customers.

'What place you want? My bus go quick-quick on that road,' the book-man grinned engagingly as Ata climbed into a green and yellow lorry with the motto, 'Fear Eats the Soul,' and Comfort followed. There was no more room and the book-man banged up the back. At first there didn't seem to be anywhere to sit in the crowded tumult under the canvas, market-women all with babies on their backs and baskets of oranges to sell, hens and ducks with their legs tied together. Then a cooking stove was shifted so Ata and Comfort could sit down.

'Me very good driver, very safe, quick-quick,' the driver sang out exuberantly as he swung the lorry onto the road. Everyone was talking and laughing and Comfort, warmed and encouraged by the noise and chatter, tried to follow.

The lorry began to climb away from the town and Comfort looking down saw a sheer drop on one side of the road and turned her head quickly away. The driver seemed to notice it at the same moment and the lorry swung wildly across the road and back and everybody screamed and then laughed with relief as the driver demonstrated both his driving skill and his intention to spice their journey with danger.

The mist had cleared and below lay the flat red plain which stretched away to a fringe of palm trees and a wide line of white surf where waves, high as houses, rolled endlessly in from their journey across the Atlantic ocean. But then the lorry turned the corner and the sea was gone, instead a steep green wall of forest where Comfort could see yellow mangoes and green pawpaw hanging from trees. At least there was food everywhere, food you could pick and eat.

'What's my grandmother like?' she asked.

'Like?' Ata laughed as if she found the question curious. 'Your grandmother has been wanting to see you for a long time.'

'I've been wanting to see her for a long time too,' Comfort said politely. 'But I mean what is she *like*?' She had learned from Winnie that people here didn't bother much with differences of personality. You were young or old, rich or poor, Ga or Fante tribe, schooled or un-schooled, such tangible things defined your status and that was that.

'Aye-aye, what sort of question is that?' Ata said half-scolding, but seeing Comfort's downcast face she added kindly, 'Your grandmother did not go to school, so how can she be book-clever like Mante? But she is money clever with her own lorry and market trade in cloth and plenty of cocoa farms. Every year farmers borrow money on their land and when they cannot pay the money back, your grandmother gets their cocoa farms instead.' Ata's laugh rumbled inside her and then exploded boisterous and joyful. 'Aye-aye, your grandmother is cocoa-farm-clever, eh?'

'Aye-aye, cocoa-farm-clever is best.' Everybody in the lorry shared the joke. 'Does anansi, the wily spider, need books?'

Comfort laughed uneasily, feeling rather sorry for the cocoa-farmers. Was she money-clever, she wondered, she had sold sweets quite as well as Winnie and in the faraway London days she had certainly made the house-keeping money go further. 'How old is my cousin, Ama?'

'Same age as you, a year older maybe,' Ata said vaguely. They had been travelling for an hour and a half when they were flagged down. A policeman frowned into the back of the lorry, counting the number of passengers ostentatiously on his fingers and finding five more than the regulations allowed. The driver explained how his passengers had begged for places and his big heart couldn't refuse, how he had eight children to feed and four nephews at school. There were tears on his cheeks as he dropped on his knees in the middle of the road, play-acting his despair and half-enjoying the situation. In the back of the lorry his passengers joined the drama, gesticulating wildly as they explained.

'Is it all right now?' Comfort said puzzled when a

moment later the driver brushed his knees and the lorry moved on.

'The driver dashed him,' Ata said.

'Oh, I see,' said Comfort used to the dash by this time. Further down the road the driver stopped and lay down along the cabin seat and declared he was too tired to drive on. Money was collected from the passengers to cover the dash and a little more and the journey continued.

Comfort had never been as tired as the evening she followed Ata down the sandy track that lead to Wanwangeri the following day. The village was not so very far from Accra but for every hour they had spent actually travelling they had spent two or three in lorry parks, drinking orange and eating roasted plantain, waiting in the shade of trees for the next lorry to fill up. Ata showed no impatience. She was used to it and enjoyed greeting friends and exchanging gossip. When it grew hot she spread her cloth and lay down with her bundle under her head and went to sleep.

'Are we nearly there?' Comfort said. They had had to walk from Akwapawa and her neck ached from the case and her feet were sore.

'Soon-soon we come to your grandmother's compound,' Ata said walking ahead down the narrow track. Between the trees Comfort could see huts and fences made of palm fronds, dried brown and brittle in the sun. Skinny cats and small white chickens scattered in front of them and children stared.

Ata turned towards a fence which was higher than its neighbouring fences and pushed her way through and Comfort followed. Inside it was like another smaller village, a dozen huts made of red swish, each one belonging to a different member of the family. One hut was used as a kitchen and the children were all gathered round, watching hungrily as the evening meal, the main meal of the day was cooked by Esi on a kerosene stove. As soon as they saw Ata, they ran round her, clapping and jumping, her own children and the children of Esi, her sister. For a moment Comfort seemed forgotten but as the hubbub subsided Ata said, 'I have brought Comfort, child of Mante.'

'Welcome, Comfort,' the ten children gazed at her round-eyed and the smaller ones pressed forward to touch her hands. The older ones went to school in neat uniforms, but at home they wore ancient shorts or cloths wound round their waists. Several had livid pink patches on their legs where cuts had festered but they all smiled widely.

'Ama, take care of Comfort,' Ata said. She stood holding her youngest child, a five year old called Bolo on her hip.

'Come,' Ama said detaching herself from the younger children and leading Comfort into one of the huts. Inside, the thatched roof was high and sloped steeply which made it surprisingly cool. There were sleeping mats rolled and stacked against the wall, a hook from which hung a mirror, several low carved stools but no other furniture except a box against the wall in which Ama kept her clothes. Comfort put her striped case beside it, carefully.

'Where is my grandmother?' she asked in Ga.

'She stays in her hut and sleeps when it it hot,' Ama said. A small girl came to the door carrying a cup of drinking water from the round calabash between her two hands and stood watching as Comfort drank it. The water was cool and tasted slightly of wood ash. 'Is she my cousin too?' Comfort said as the child scampered away.

'Tawia?' Ama seemed surprised and held up her fingers to explain. 'She is your sister like I am your sister. Our mother and your father are brother and sister so of course we are sisters too, that way there is peace and happiness in the family.'

'Oh, I see,' said Comfort pleased to find Ama was her *sister*, that according to this reckoning she had lots of

brothers and sisters. Ama squatted on her heels beside Comfort's case. She was a year older than Comfort and a shade taller, her breasts small bumps under her cloth. Her hair was short and her eyes wide, she had small gold earrings like Comfort's own. 'Is your father's hut here too?'

'Of course not,' Ama snorted with merriment. 'He lives in the men's compound. How can a man talk wisely if he lives with children who chatter like monkeys? It is good you come here, very good. We talk every night before we go to sleep, yes?' Ama's smile was open and completely friendly. 'You tell me about England, yes, and I tell you about Wanwangeri and which boys are nice, yes? For a long time my sister, Yaa, Esi's daughter, slept in this hut with me but now she is married and gone to her husband's village. Aye-aye, I was sad that day but now you come and I am glad. We will go to the market together each day?'

'Don't you go to school?' Comfort asked.

'School?' Ama laughed. 'I am thirteen years old, how can I go to school with so many children here, water to fetch, food to cook?' She talked in the same dramatic way as her mother, gesturing with her hands. 'Besides I must go to the market with my mother or Esi and there is much to learn before I am fit to be a woman.'

'Which is Grandmother's hut?' Comfort asked twisting the amulet that hung round her neck. Ama pointed to a hut made of red swish like the others but with a pattern of wide black and white bands painted on the outside walls and a curtain of plastic ribbons across the doorway instead of a sack. Outside Esi called that the food was ready and began scooping it from the big cooking pots into bowls.

'Come, you will see Grandmother now and I must take food to my father,' Ama said. Wives took it in turns to cook for their husbands and daughters carried the food across. Ama took the first bowl and disappeared out of the gate and the younger girl, Tawia, took the next bowl and followed Ama out. Everyone was served in a particular order according to their age, Bolo was one of the smallest and he and the other children waited patiently though their eyes watched the food. Esi handed two bowls to Comfort.

'Give this to Grandmother,' she said.

'Suppose she is still asleep?' Comfort murmured shyly but Grandmother was already coming out of her hut. She looked older than Comfort had imagined and she was taller too. Her face was thin, hawk-like as she stood leaning on her stick and staring at Comfort with bright black eyes.

'Aye-aye, my been-to granddaughter has come at last,' she muttered in Ga, she spoke no English, and sighed with a deep satisfaction as if something was at last completed. 'An only palm fruit does not get lost in the fire.'

'Greetings to you, Grandmother. I have been wanting to see you for a long time. Thank you for the amulet, it has brought me good luck already if it has brought me here to see you,' Comfort said, aware that this was an important moment. She spoke in the way Mante had taught her. The words were waiting ready on her tongue.

'Aye-aye, the child speaks well. She is truly Mante's child. Were there not always plenty of sweet words in Mante's mouth?' her grandmother inquired of the compound.

'My father sends his greetings. He hopes to visit you soon,' Comfort added.

'Pshaw, greetings cost nothing,' Grandmother said settling herself on one of the stools in front of her hut and waving Comfort to sit on another. 'Now eat, child.'

Comfort was hungry. There had been plenty of snacks and drinks during the journey to Wanwangeri but it was the first solid meal she had had in two days. She had never eaten *kenke* before but now she broke a bit from the soft white lump with her fingers and scooped it into the meat and vegetable stew under her grandmother's critical gaze.

'Aye-aye, Mante's child eats with her fingers, eh?' she said with a derisive chuckle and she began to eat herself, rolling her *kenke* delicately into a ball the size of a chestnut before she dipped it in the stew. Was that the correct way, Comfort wondered, watching carefully and doing the same. It was quiet in the compound then. Talking at meal times was bad manners and such bad manners could make your father die. The ten children ate in silence, washing their bowls when they had finished and slipping out of the compound.

Grandmother finished eating and closed her eyes. She seemed to be asleep with her back propped against the wall of the hut. Could she slip away now, Comfort wondered. She wanted to talk to Ama and see the rest of Wanwangeri but every time she stirred her grandmother stirred too. The sun sank behind the palm trees and shadows lengthened and the boys carried their father's stools to the shade tree in the centre of the village where everybody met and talked. Only Esi and Ata sat gossiping quietly in the corner near the kitchen, each with a small child asleep on her lap.

Comfort stood up and Grandmother opened her eyes at once, 'I worked for Mante day and night, paying for his schooling, my youngest son,' Grandmother said. 'Is it the will of Onyame that a child send his mother a blue letter from England to break her heart?'

'What blue letter?' Comfort whispered.

'What blue letter?' Grandmother repeated rocking backwards and forwards as she remembered her sadness. 'The blue letter which tells that he has married a white woman in that London place. A father and mother must choose a bride first time, what can a young man know of such things? How can we find out if the girl is healthy and respectable and can cook as a wife should cook? A child was born in London and lost to us,' Grandmother hugged her arms tight across her chest and her eyes circled the quiet compound, rested a moment on Ata and Esi and the sleeping children and came back to Comfort. Beyond the palm-frond fence there was drumming now, a soft throbbing that was part of the Wanwangeri darkness.

'But now that child has come,' Grandmother said softly. 'How can a son stand against Onyame and his own mother? At last you have come to me, Comfort.'

8

Early sun light was streaming round the sack at the doorway. 'When can I go to the market in Akwapawa?' Comfort wrote in her diary on December 5th, pressing hard and dark. She blinked up at the shadowy slope of the thatch above her. The struts which supported it were riddled with black termite holes, nothing made of wood lasted long in Wanwangeri, even her plastic suitcase had termite holes. The yellow dresses were faded to ivory and torn now from frequent washings and Comfort was aware of more subtle changes too, changes in how she thought and what she believed. What she wanted now was to go to the market and Grandmother wouldn't allow it. 'If a little bird talks like a big bird it may hurt itself with the sound of its own voice,' Grandmother said cryptically.

Comfort kept quite still on her sleeping mat, knowing that as soon as she stirred, Ama would wake and the day would begin. A chicken came pecking in under the sack and paused as if it half-expected her to shoo it out. Comfort blew gently in its direction, raising a tiny red dust storm and flattening its feathers on its scrawny neck. She had been at Wanwangeri for more than a month but days rather than dates were important here. Friday was the birthday of the land and no farming was done. How could you dig the earth on its birthday, Ama said, and Comfort agreed such a thing was impossible. Tuesday was the birthday of the sea and no fishing could be done.

Already Comfort was used to living in Wanwangeri, used to her grandmother's eyes, bright between wrinkled lids, following her everywhere with an expression she could not fathom. Grandmother had been very pleased by her arrival, it was Comfort who sat on the stool close by her and Comfort's shoulder she clutched if she walked in the village. Comfort was soothed and warmed by this extra attention, closeness she had not had since Margaret died, but once she heard Ata and Esi grumbling together at the way Grandmother favoured her above their own children.

There was drumming and dancing nearly every evening in the centre of the village. Ama was teaching her the intricate steps of the *adowa*, a slow graceful dance.

Dancing was not a matter of choice, the drumming called to Comfort's feet, commanded them to dance. The whole village danced and on feast days the drumming and dancing went on all night. Children died and crops failed and farms were lost but the dancing still went on. Comfort was used now to the drumming and dancing and used to groundnut stew eaten with fufu and the constant feel of grit between her toes. Her sandals wore out and were not replaced, nobody talked of hookworm here and besides Comfort always wore her amulet. The soles of her feet grew hard though she was still careful where she put them. A scorpion bite was very bad luck, Ama said. Mosquitoes whined in the darkness. On Hillside Estate Comfort had been given anti-malarial pills but here fevers were cured by the fetish priest with spells and herb medicines and sometimes with penicillin. If the priest failed there was a clinic at Akwapawa.

Comfort knew the village now, who everybody was and who was related to whom. She knew Sika, the headman who settled disputes and who treated Grandmother with the marked respect due to her age and the lorry she owned. She knew Tete, who played the drums, sending messages to the next village as clearly as any radio. Once she and Ama had seen a bright green snake curling round a branch. Ama had shouted and some men came with sticks and killed it. It was very unlucky indeed to be bitten by a green mamba, Ama said, you might easily die, but the grey and orange lizards which scuttled in the dust everywhere, would do you no harm.

Everybody in Wanwangeri greeted Comfort with wide smiles. 'Aye-aye, Mante's daughter from England,' they said at first admiring the lightness of her skin. But now they were used to her and being in the sun all day she was almost as dark as the other girls in the village. Sometimes she thought of Mante and wondered when she was going back. If she was ever going back. But it would be ungracious to ask such a question in Grandmother's compound when everybody had done their best to welcome her. All Comfort wanted now was to get to the market at Akwapawa.

'I shall ask Grandmother about the market today,' Comfort said when Ama woke. Saying it was easy but doing it would not be because Grandmother liked ideas to come from herself and often got angry. And there were so many rules about a younger person properly addressing an older person that it was hard to say anything without breaking them.

'Perhaps better to wait a bit,' Ama mumbled as both girls went to wash from the cold bucket at the back of the compound, scrubbing themselves all over with soap and palm-frond. You would have bad luck all day if you did not wash as soon as you left your sleeping mat, Ama said.

'But I have waited a long time already,' Comfort said scooping the cold water from the bucket and shivering as it slid down her body taking off the soap. 'I could wait for ever.'

'There are worse things than waiting,' Ama said. Waiting was something she accepted fatalistically, waiting was part of life. Ama was her friend now, the best of sisters, Comfort thought, and she tried hard to be patient like Ama.

After they had washed the two girls went to the tap with buckets on their heads. It was their job to fill the tub in the compound each morning and wash the younger children. Comfort washed Bolo and dressed him in uniform ready for school. She no longer thought of school for herself. She was nearly as old as Ama and besides wandering close to the school-house and hearing the pupils chanting their seven times table, she did not want to go.

As Comfort cleaned the cooking place, daubing white clay along it, she rehearsed what to say to Grandmother. The compound was quiet, Ata and Ama had already left and the little ones were playing with a pile of coca-cola tins when the plastic ribbons quivered and Grandmother came from her hut. She paused a moment blinking in the sun.

'Good morning, Grandmother, I hope you slept well,' Comfort said determined to speak before her courage failed. A direct request would not be polite, a delicate subject had to be approached in a roundabout way. 'Ama and Ata have gone to Akwapawa.'

'The market starts early,' Grandmother replied in the same vein, though there was a challenging gleam in her eyes now.

'Can I go to the market with them tomorrow?' Comfort asked suddenly incautious. What good did it do, trying to be patient.

'*You* go to market?' Grandmother struck the ground angrily with her stick. 'How can you go to market when you do not even know how to speak politely to your own grandmother? You will disgrace us all with your forward manners. Besides you are too young. A child cracks the shell of a snail but not that of the tortoise.'

'But I am nearly as old as Ama,' Comfort mumbled.

'Aye-aye, the child argues, what behaviour is this?' Grandmother addressed the compound and then her eyes shining black like stones in a stream-bed, swung back to Comfort. In the corner the children had stopped playing and watched her stick ready to dart. 'Ama knows how to speak to her elders and how to make *abomu* and *garri* too. A girl who does not know such things brings shame on her family. When you can make abomu then we will talk of going to the market.'

'It's not fair,' Comfort said but the anger in her grandmother's eyes dried the words in her throat. She ran to her hut, scattering the children and chickens, flinging herself down on her sleeping mat and beating with her fists against the iron-hard ground. But her fury passed and it was dull lying by herself in the hut and she could hear the children playing again and the chickens pecking in the dust and when Esi called her to fetch more water Comfort came out. 'Please will you teach me to make abomu,' she whispered hanging her head and hoping nobody would hear.

'Aye-aye, tomorrow we will make abomu, daughter,' Esi said loudly. She turned laughing to the rest of the compound and in the corner the children laughed too and a single dry cackle came from the shadows of Grandmother's hut.

All the next day Comfort made abomu, washing and chopping the vegetables, cooking and pounding them with bits of fish and onion and red palm-oil. How could any cooking be worth so much trouble when it wasn't even for a party, Comfort thought. But the abomu was good. Praises came back from the men's compound when Ama and Tawia carried the bowls to their fathers and little Bolo smiled like a slice of melon and said it was the best abomu he had ever tasted.

'Did my granddaughter, Comfort, make this abomu?' Grandmother said pretending surprise. 'Aye-aye, it is been-to abomu then?' The laughter which rippled round the compound was not entirely friendly. Why should this granddaughter from England be always at her grand-mother's side, hearing all that passed. The chicken which is nearer its mother eats the thigh of the grass-hopper. Such a book-clever girl could learn too much. The harmattan season had begun in December, Sahara winds dried the trees which cracked loud as guns and tempers frayed.

Comfort's abomu was eaten for breakfast and at midday next day. A quantity of food was always cooked so that the women were free to go to the market or attend to their farms. Comfort did not ask if she could go to the market again but when the abomu was finished Grand-mother took a cloth out of the box in her hut.

'A girl who can make abomu so well must wear African cloth,' she said. The cloth had blue and orange circles floating like balloons in a cream-coloured sky.

'Thank you, Grandmother,' Comfort smiled. Ata sewed the cloth for her and now Comfort was dressed as Ama was dressed, now surely she would be allowed to go to the market but she did not ask.

'Aye-aye, so smart you look, gay as a pineapple,' Grandmother said. 'Do you like the cloth I gave you?'

'Yes, Grandmother, thank you, I like it very much,' Comfort said. The old yellow dresses were used as rags and Comfort went on waiting patiently and hoping. But there was still no mention of the market.

'Go and help Esi with her farm,' Grandmother said a few days later. 'And if you work well, soon you shall have a farm of your own.'

'Thank you, Grandmother,' Comfort said dully. She realised then that the cloth was *instead* of the market and the farm was instead of the market too but she did not

run off to her hut this time. *Fair* and *not fair* were no use in Wanwangeri, Comfort stopped even thinking about what Margaret said.

Starting the farm was a special occasion which began with a ceremony two weeks later when the harmattan was over. Ata and Esi and their husbands and children followed Grandmother out of the village to the patch, twelve metres square, which was to be Comfort's farm, singing as they went. The singing stirred something inside Comfort. Grandmother asked Onyame's permission for her granddaughter to use the land which really belonged to him and as she poured the palm-wine into the soil, turning it red as blood, Comfort felt part of herself soak into the earth forever. Her mouth was dry as sand. After that she worked on the farm every day, digging long furrows with the short thick hoe they used in Wanwangeri and planting yam and sweet potatoes and pawpaw seeds which sprouted into tiny trees in less than a week.

It was January when the letter came. There were no letters delivered to the village but Ata brought this one from the post office in Akwapawa. 'Read it to me, child, Mante's writing goes across the page like the march of ants,' Grandmother said not caring to admit she could neither read nor write. Comfort read the letter slowly. A son had been born two weeks before, a strong boy-child *out-doored* already on the eighth day according to custom, and due to be christened next week, Jeo chosen for Mante's family, Peter chosed by Efua.

'Jeo,' murmured Grandmother happily and her eyes filled with tears as she called. 'My son, Mante, has a son called Jeo.' Comfort read on silently, Mante hoped Comfort was behaving well, repaying his mother for the money she had spent on him and the pain and disappointment he had caused her. That he did not mention her return was no surprise to Comfort because she had known for a long time that she was not expected back at Hillside Estate.

The news of Jeo's birth flew round the village and all

110

that evening Grandmother sat in front of her hut receiving best wishes and congratulations. Ama and Comfort served drink and food to all the well-wishers but when the compound was quiet at last and the moon high and white in the sky, Comfort whispered 'When can I go to the market, Grandmother?'

'Aye-aye, always wanting something,' Grandmother said irritably, she was worn out with so many visitors. She wanted to keep Comfort always at her side. This granddaughter she never expected to see, would be the eyes and ears of her old age once she had learned the customs, a spirited child, quick to learn, just as she had been herself. Hadn't Onyame answered her prayers at last? 'Can you make garri yet? When you can make garri we will talk about the market.'

Three days later the garri was made and stored away in a sack like white sand. That evening Ama was late back from the market and Ata asked Comfort to carry the food to Ama's father, Obodai, in the men's compound. Comfort followed Tawia down the path with the bowl of palm-nut stew.

'Obodai, father of Ama, I bring you food,' Comfort said keeping her eyes politely on the ground as she handed him the bowl. She knew Obodai well, he often came to visit Ata and play with his children. Half an hour later she collected the bowl. The men had already gone to sit under the shade tree but a piece of meat, red with palm-oil lay in the bottom of Obodai's bowl.

'How wasteful he is,' Comfort said.

'Not wasteful,' Tawia said scooping a similar titbit from the bottom of the other bowl. 'He has left it for you because you carried his food. Come on, Grandmother wants you to hurry, the lorry driver has come.'

'Thank you, Obodai,' Comfort murmured as Tawia ran off but though the portions of meat in Grandmother's compound were not large she flicked the morsel onto the ground where a chicken grabbed it. Obadai wasn't her father after all.

'Business is bad,' the lorry driver was saying in a doleful voice. Grandmother blinked at the pieces of paper he had put in her lap and then handed them to Comfort. Comfort could make no sense of the scribbled figures about kilometres and litres of petrol but she could feel Grandmother's eyes upon the back of her neck.

'How many kilometres do you travel on one litre of petrol?' she asked at last.

'Spare parts are *kalabule*, black market,' the driver said rolling his eyes uneasily. 'Very expensive. A lorry in bad repair uses plenty of petrol. This Comfort is a fine girl,' he added to Grandmother with an ingratiating smile.

'She has come from England to help me with my trade,' Grandmother said. 'I am fortunate in my family. As we say in Ghana, A man who lives on a river bank should not wash his hands with spittle.'

'Well said indeed. When a single tree faces the fury of the storm it is blown down,' the lorry driver responded. 'But the tree in the forest survives. Let us hope the lorry shows a better profit soon, Onyame willing.'

'Is something wrong with the lorry?' Comfort asked frowning over the figures after he had gone.

'Aye-aye, I am a poor old woman,' Grandmother said hugging her arms across her chest and rocking back and forth. 'If I had a son to drive my lorry there would be no cheating but my son works in the modern world and forgets the old ways. I am just an old sponge to be used in times of need.'

'Maybe when I am older I can drive the lorry for you?' Comfort said.

'Can a tortoise fly?' Grandmother said crushingly. 'A woman can own a lorry but whoever heard of a woman driving one?'

'Everything changes,' Comfort said. She was beginning to understand her grandmother. 'If I went to the market I could watch the lorry and the driver for you.'

'You talk too much,' Grandmother snapped. 'It is not the custom for girls to talk so freely.'

'Sorry,' Comfort murmured eyes on the ground, but she was growing wily now just as Grandmother was wily. 'Sorry, sorry, sorry.'

'You speak well and learn fast,' Grandmother said after a pause. 'You are a true child of this family and tomorrow you shall go to the market in Akwapawa.'

'As Onyame wills,' Comfort murmured.

9

Comfort settled on a wooden box behind the stall and gazed across Akwapawa market. At last she had got herself to the market there where she wanted to be, just as she had got herself into Ghana. The shrill tumult rang in her ears. There was a concrete floor and high above her head a corrugated iron roof supported on green-painted pillars mottled with rust. There were dozens of stalls under the roof and outside its protection there were women sitting with baskets as far as the eye could see. Hundreds of women who simply laid their goods out on the ground, oranges, yams, cassava, tomatoes and lettuces grown on their own farms, cloth, soap and plastic combs bought to trade.

Everything was round, round woven baskets like cottage loaves, round head-scarves circled the heads of married women, round fruit in round piles, round bumps of babies tied to their mothers' backs. The market women themselves were round too as they settled like plump pears on the ground beside their goods, *bottom power* it was called, the power of the market mammies. Even the patterns on their cloths were round, Ata's had round yellow leaves on a black ground, Abla's at the next stall had scarlet vines with round dark-blue fruits, balloons floated on Comfort's.

The hubbub bounced against the roof and echoed back, morning greetings, babies crying, lorries revving, the shout of book-men and the cries of the market women calling to possible customers, their voices falling with a lower price as the customer walked away showing a real or feigned lack of interest.

'And who is this then?' Abla shouted above the din and her smile flashed white. She had a baby sleeping on her back and two small children playing on the ground beside her.

'Comfort, child of my brother, Mante,' Ata said but her eyes were anxious as she settled Bolo on a bed of cloth under the stall. Bolo was feverish. The fetish priest had given medicine but the child seemed no better.

'Ah, Comfort who comes from England,' Abla said. 'No wonder she stares like an owl caught in the daylight. The stranger has big eyes but does not see what is happening.' Comfort smiled gently to herself. She was surely no stranger who was allowed to come to Akwana-wa market to watch Grandmother's lorry as well as learn to trade in cloth.

'I have brought the medicine,' Abla said handing a bottle of spinach-green liquid to Ata. 'My son, Dublo, had a fever and bad leg just the same as Bolo and now he is well, Onyame be praised. Dublo hold out your leg.' There was a grey scar patch where the sore had healed . Many of the children round the market had such grey scars.

'How much do I owe you?' Ata said pouring a large dose into a cup for Bolo.

'Pay me when the child is well,' Abla said with a shrug. Most of the stalls sold the same goods, competing with each other but the competition stayed friendly.

Trading was only part of market life and the market women were almost a family in themselves, a friendly society helping each other in time of trouble, a force to be reckoned with.

'Come and buy my cloth, fine-fine cloth,' Ata called as the market filled and the sun rose high in the sky. Her eyes searched the passing faces for likely customers. 'Fine cloth. Very cheap price.'

'What is the *right* price for cloth?' Comfort asked, trying to follow Ata's movements and do exactly as she did. The price called seemed to vary with every customer.

'Aye-aye, you will soon learn how it is,' Ata said. 'The price depends how a person looks, whether he or she is well-dressed and prosperous, a cheerful face will pay a better price.'

'I see,' said Comfort not quite sure that she did.

'But you have to be very careful,' Ata explained. 'We market mammies of Ghana are very powerful people according to the government. They blame us when the price rises. Now prices are fixed by law, everyone must sell at the fixed price but there is always a dash as well and the dash is not fixed.'

'But . . . .' said Comfort still not sure she understood. It sounded like a trick.

'People do not always want to buy at first,' Ata explained. 'You have to hook them like fish in the river, persuade them how cheap the cloth is, you will soon learn how it is done. Look after the stall while I see when the clinic opens.'

'But I . . . .' Comfort began but Ata was already making her way across the crowded market and in Ghana people did not care for too many questions. For a

moment Comfort watched her aunt and then she smiled down at Bolo, his eyes shone very bright under the stall.

'Very nice cloth,' Comfort muttered and a woman passing in a blue print frock turned her head and glanced curiously. 'Come and buy my very nice cloth.'

'Louder,' whispered Bolo. 'You sound like a small frog croaking in a dry pond.'

'Come buy my cloth. Very fine cloth,' Comfort called and this time several heads turned and at the next stall Abla laughed.

'Aye-aye, Comfort has found her voice,' she said, suckling her baby now but continuing to call to customers. 'The green fruit ripens fast.'

And Comfort had found her voice. 'Come buy my cloth. This is very fine cloth,' she chanted like the others and soon she was making up new calls too, partly to entertain Bolo. 'Buy this cloth and you will look as gay as a pineapple.' A small snicker of laughter came from under the stall. In Grandmother's compound Comfort had to be so careful what she said and the freedom of the market was very exciting. Here you had to push and shout and grab to survive.

'You call like an oriole bird already,' Bolo muttered as she leant down and gave him a drink from the bottle of orange. His forehead seemed very hot and there was a sour smell about him, white clay was smeared round a deep cut on his leg. Comfort took Grandmother's amulet from her neck and put it round Bolo's. It was all she could do. Hadn't it kept her safe and well, perhaps it would help him. There was a note of desperation in her voice as she called now. Nobody seemed to realise how sick Bolo was. A woman stopped and fingered a cloth patterned with orange, brown and black diamond-shapes like a snake skin.

'How much? she asked.

'Well, two hundred cedis,' Comfort said snatching the first price which came into her head. It was a high price she knew but the woman looked both prosperous and cheerful. 'Just to you this cloth is two hundred cedis.'

'Two hundred cedis is far too high,' said the woman sharply. 'You will land yourself in prison charging such prices. If I report you to the people's court you will be certainly fined and quite right too.'

'To you it's fifty cedis, I made a mistake,' Comfort said hastily, her stomach turning to a hard cold lump. How she hated it when people got angry. Everything changed when people got angry. 'It is a fine-fine cloth and will suit you well. See how it brings out the brightness of your eyes and the snake smoothness of your skin.'

'What?' said the woman loudly. 'Are you telling me that I am like a snake? You have too much to say for yourself. The fixed price for a cloth like this is thirty cedis.' She turned away.

'Thirty cedis then,' Comfort called after her. 'You can have the cloth for thirty cedis.'

'Now we are getting somewhere,' the woman said coming back. She was smiling now, she seemed quite pleased with the bargain. Comfort did not know whether to be proud of her first sale or not as she wrapped the cloth in a piece of brown paper and the woman walked away.

'I have sold the snake-pattern cloth,' Comfort said when Ata returned. 'For thirty cedis, the fixed price.'

'And did you get the dash too, what was the dash?' Ata asked her eyes lack-lustre.

'No dash, I forgot,' Comfort said.

'Aye-aye, you must learn our ways quick-quick or you will make beggars of us all,' Ata said but she was half-abstracted as she gazed down at Bolo who had fallen asleep. The clinic would be open later, she would take Bolo over then but already dozens of children were waiting. 'Didn't I tell you that each cloth has a fixed price because the government says so but you must ask for a dash as well?'

'Sorry,' said Comfort very cast down. She was half-Ghanaian but sometimes she wondered if she would ever get things right. 'Sorry.'

In the afternoon Ata carried Bolo to the clinic on her back like a cloth baby and when she brought him back his leg had been covered with white bandage and he had been given pills. Ata tipped the pills, white and gritty, into her palm and sniffed them doubtfully. Nobody had told her what kinds of pills they were, she only knew they were expensive. Already her eyes were glazed with sadness. Every day children got sick and went back to their sky-families, she accepted such an outcome fatalistically since too much hope and struggle would only cause further pain. It was the will of Onyame.

'How did you get on at the market, Comfort?' Grandmother asked when they got back. 'Come and sit beside me and tell me all about it.'

'I sold a cloth,' Comfort muttered. 'But I sold it for the fixed price and no dash.'

'Which cloth?' asked Grandmother who knew every one of the cloths in her stock and remembered the details of each sale for five years back.

'The one with little diamonds of orange and black, the one like snake skin.'

'Aye-aye, she sold it for thirty cedis and no dash,' Ata said and even Ama smiled at such simplicity. She had been eager for Comfort to go to the market but that day she had had to stay behind and help Esi with the cooking and Ama had not liked that.

'Aye-aye, the child has to learn. The fledgling eagle will soar to the sky soon enough,' Grandmother said.

'I saw your lorry this afternoon, Grandmother,' Comfort whispered later in the evening. Everyone had eaten then and Grandmother sat with her eyes closed. Outside Tete was drumming under a starry sky and the others had gone off to join the evening dancing. Only Ata stayed in her hut with Bolo and his father Obodai.

'Are you sure,' Grandmother said and her eyes clicked open wide. 'What colour was it? How did you know it was my lorry?'

'I saw the motto, "DRY LEAF FALL" written on the bonnet,' Comfort said anxious to make up for her failure with the cloth. 'And the colour was yellow as bananas and green as limes. And I saw the driver sleeping in the cabin too.'

'Sleeping, what is this sleeping?' Grandmother said. 'The lorry eats petrol like a worm-ridden goat but makes no profit, yet the driver sleeps.' Her stick swept round the empty compound. 'All these children, their fathers pay for their food but who is to pay for their schooling and books? Mante has a son of his own and a modern wife who must have modern air that comes from a cold box. Aye-aye, is there no end to the tricks people play, the misfortunes of a poor old woman?' Behind them Bolo turned on his mat and moaned. Obodai left quickly to find the fetish priest.

'I will never trick you, Grandmother,' Comfort whispered. 'And I am sorry I sold the cloth too cheap.'

'Aye-aye, you are young yet,' Grandmother said and she patted Comfort's hand. 'The child breaks the snail shell but not the tortoise shell. But you shall be my eyes and ears, Comfort, it is the will of Onyame.'

'Onyame?' Comfort murmured, Was it the will of Onyame that had brought her to Wanwangeri, she wondered. Were his will and Grandmother's always exactly the same. For a moment she listened to the drumming and clapping of hands and thud of feet as Wanwangeri danced. Comfort wanted to dance too and Grandmother's eyes had closed again but her hand clutched tight on Comfort's arm. If she was Grandmother's eyes and ears she would have to stay in Wanwangeri for a long time. And if she stayed for a long time, she might have to stay for ever. Comfort stared at the patch of light thrown by the pressure lamp and wrote in the red dust with her foot, *Bolo*. It was a long time since she had written anything and a very long time since she had written her diary. What month was it now she wondered.

There was a strange sound, a moan which rose to a scream so wild that Comfort imagined an animal, a leopard had come into the compound. The drumming stopped abruptly. Comfort leapt to her feet and as the sound died away, she realised the scream had come from Ata's hut.

'Bolo,' Grandmother whispered. 'Both the green leaf and the dry leaf fall. Bolo has gone to his sky-family, such a good beautiful child, they let him come to us but now they have taken him back.' Her eyes were still closed but tears trickled from the corners, tears for Bolo and for all the children and grand-children she had lost. Many children died every year in Wanwangeri.

Once Comfort had started at the market in Akwapawa Grandmother seemed eager for her to go there every day and a new life started. Comfort was good at selling and though the times were difficult, trade at Grandmother's stall was better than most. For several weeks Ata stayed at home, grieving long after Bolo was buried, the libations poured and the ceremonies performed. Now she preferred the quiet routine of cooking and caring for the younger children to the hurly-burly of the market. Now it was Esi and Comfort who went to the market and sometimes Ama. But Ama was quieter now too. Was she grieving for Bolo too, Comfort wondered. At first the two girls had talked late into the night and Ama had been eager to tell Comfort all about the village but now she seemed dreamy and even sullen. She wandered off by herself and gathered red hisbiscus flowers and tucked them into her cloth.

Comfort was used to market now, adapted to it just as she had adapted to different schools and enjoyed it hugely. She knew everybody and everybody knew her. Every day she invented new calls, different calls. 'Buy my cloth and soon you will be Beauty Queen of Akwapawa,' Comfort shouted running after a customer. 'Buy my cloth and every fridgeful man in Akwapawa will ask to marry you.' The other girls in the market listened and copied.

'Aye-aye, stay at the stall and keep quiet,' Esi scolded her and even complained to Grandmother. But Grandmother seemed quite pleased. 'My granddaughter is trade-clever, business-clever, just as I was. We need a trade-clever girl in this family.'

All morning Comfort looked after the cloth stall but by mid-day it was too hot to work and then Esi and Comfort dozed in such shade as they could find. In the late afternoon Comfort wandered round the market. She spoke Ga as well as anybody now and could make herself understood in Twi and Hausa too. She flitted through the market sometimes with Abla's baby tied on her back, minding stalls for those with no daughters and writing letters for people who could not write. One day Grandmother's lorry was waiting for hours while the driver and book-man drank palm-wine at the other side of the market. The driver's eyes rolled with alarm when he visited Grandmother at Wanwangeri. How did she know of his palm-wine days unless it was from magic or witchcraft? After that the lorry covered more kilometres and carried more people but its hunger for petrol was miraculously less.

And Comfort began trading on her own account with the dashes she got for writing letters and minding stalls and the money from the red handbag. She changed the English pounds into cedis at a shop beside the market too and bought talcum powder and soap and carried them in a basket on her head.

One day she stopped beside a shiny blue car and stared with a group of children at the white couple getting out.

'Buy my soap, fine-fine soap,' Comfort shouted suddenly darting forward and automatically pushing the basket in front of them.

'No thanks,' the woman spoke in English and Comfort felt a strange clawing in her chest and walked down the street after them.

'That girl is following us?' the woman muttered.

'Hoping to sell us something I suppose,' the man turned and spoke in loud clear tones. 'Run along now, we are not going to buy anything.'

'Do you come from London?' Comfort said softly. The English words sounded strange, like clothes put away in mothballs. It was so long since she had used them.

'What? Yes, we do,' the man said speaking slowly and carefully. 'You learn English at school? You speak it well.'

'Of course I do,' Comfort muttered smiling. 'I'm half-English. My granny is English in England.'

'Oh yes?' the man said pausing a moment, eyebrows raised.

'It could be true,' the woman said. 'Her English is very good for school English.'

'If you believe that you'll believe anything,' the man said walking on.

'What month is it?' Comfort called.

'March,' the woman said. 'Almost April.'

10

'Comfort, wake up, you must fetch my mother,' Ama whispered and her words dragged Comfort from a deep pit of sleep. Sun was already streaming in round the sack at the doorway.

'What?' Comfort said turning her head. Ama was sitting with her knees huddled to her chest and her cloth pulled up to her face. Above it her eyes were round and shining like new coins. There was blood on her sleeping mat.

'You must fetch Ata, my mother, I cannot go out for eight days now, that is the custom,' Ama said. Comfort pulled at her own cloth and stumbled into the early morning cool. Chickens pecking in the coral dust squawked and scattered as she ran.

'Ata, Ata,' she whispered pushing the words into the dim twilight of the hut. You must always call a person's name, call their spirit back before waking them. Ata leaned up on her elbow. Her sleep had been fragile since Bolo died. The four children on their mats beside her slept on. 'Ama wants you, Ama needs you.'

Comfort did not quite know what to say but it seemed to be enough. Ata got up with a sigh, tightening her cloth as she walked across the compound, her wide hips swinging. Comfort followed slowly, hearing the two of

them, mother and daughter in the hut, voices soft as
wood pigeons. She wondered who she would call, what
she would do when her turn came.

'Take your things to the other hut,' Ata said jerking
her head towards the scatter of clothes and the trading
basket. 'The hut next to your grandmother's.'

The new hut had been used as a store but had recently
been cleared and re-thatched. What had happened had
been prepared for, Ama would have her own hut now,
that was the custom. It meant that Comfort had her own
hut too. Comfort let her sleeping-mat fall on the dust
floor, it was still warm from her body. There was water
to be fetched and the smaller children to be washed
ready for schol before she left for the market in Akwapawa.

'Is it true about Ama?' they asked at the tap, no secrets
were kept long in Wanwangeri. But there was to be no

127

market for Comfort that day or for the days that followed.

'You must stay here today,' Esi said when she returned with the bucket of water, hurrying and spilling a little in a cold trail down her back.

'Stay here?' Comfort said trying to keep the note of indignation out of her voice. She had never quite got used to doing what she was told, the frustration of not doing what she wanted. Didn't she sell cloth better than anybody. 'But why?'

'Hurry up with that water,' Esi said pouring from the bucket over the two soap-covered children. 'Is there nothing but market business in your head these days? Ama, your sister, must stay in her hut for eight days, that is the custom. Who will help with the cooking and washing if you go to the market? Besides there is yam and egg to be prepared for Ama's ceremony this afternoon.'

That morning Comfort boiled eggs and yam and pounded them into a yellow pulp. Ama sat in her hut with a cloth round her middle and her shoulders bare. She glanced at Comfort but her look was distant, her eyes like black glass, raised a barrier between them. An old woman had come to perform the ceremony and she took the dish in her hands, kneading the yam between her fingers and then brushing it against Ama's lips.

'This girl has entered womanhood today,' she said repeating the words and actions three times and then scattering the handful on the ground where chickens pecked it up. Then she handed the dish to the children who grabbed it and thrust their fingers into the yam almost as eagerly. Ama's lips moved as she counted the children eating from the dish.

'Ten,' she whispered at last and smiled a secret inward smile. As many children as ate from the dish, Ama was destined to bear and ten was a good omen. The same dreamy inward smile touched all the women's faces as libations were poured to the ancestors, and even Ata smiled that day for the first time since Bolo died.

In the evening the drumming started but Comfort sat cross-legged in her new hut. Her hands rubbed across her body slowly, feeling the new softness of her own growing breasts.

'Why do you sit in the hut in darkness?' Grandmother called from her stool outside. 'This is a day of celebration.'

'Because I have no lamp,' Comfort said sullenly but it was not the real reason. The drumming called to her feet, called to the spirit inside her, the spirit she shared with her father and all his family, but that night she had no wish to dance. She couldn't forget the English couple she had seen a few days before. They hadn't believed she was half-English, had she really changed so much, Comfort wondered.

'Aye-aye, what sort of answer is that?' Grandmother said. 'Children nowadays not a scrap of manners. There is an old lamp in the kitchen, ask Esi to give it to you.'

'Thank you, Grandmother.'

Comfort held the lamp above her head staring round the hut by its dim and flickering light. A place of your own was the best thing in the world, Margaret had said a long time ago when they played the house-game. Now, at last, Comfort had a place of her own. Her own hut. But everything changed and already there were termite holes in the wooden struts of the new thatch and little blobs of mud, wasp nests, and already the new roof was the kingdom for a thousand insects.

'Are you not pleased to have your own hut?' Grandmother's stick clicked impatiently as she stood in the doorway, silhouetted against the brighter light of her own pressure lamp. 'Your own hut and your own lamp as well? Aye-aye, the chicken which is nearer its Grandmother eats the thigh of the grass-hopper,' she added, adapting the proverb slightly for this situation.

'Yes, thank you, Grandmother,' Comfort said.

'You are younger than Ama but already you have her privileges,' Grandmother said, not quite satisfied with Comfort's answer. 'Aye-aye, young people are never content nowadays, but only the monkey can relieve the monkey's distress.' She clicked irritably away across the compound. Outside they were drumming, hands clapping, feet thudding in time to the rhythm. But there were other voices from long ago and far away. You'll make brain surgeon shouldn't wonder, (that had been a joke of course,) Comfort Jones, you've got a long way to go.

Comfort rummaged in her suitcase and found the diary. April, they had said, and the pages were empty since November and for a second she wondered if she could still write in English and then she wrote slowly. 'Do I want to stay forever in Wanwangeri?' She tied the diary on a thong and wore it round her neck under her cloth just as she had worn the amulet which she had given to Bolo. She had got herself to Ghana but the force which had brought her to Wanwangeri and was determined to keep her there, was the force of Grandmother's will. Could she stand against it now that she knew Grandmother and her fierce temper, now that she knew about the bonds that bound them and the obligations owed.

The sky was clear blue above her head all that week. There was plenty to be done in the compound and when the heat of the day was over, Comfort went out to work on her farm, breaking the baked earth with her hoe while questions filtered through her head. If she stayed much longer she would have to stay for always because she would only know about Wanwangeri and Akwapawa and the customs of the Ga people. She was restless now, just as she had been restless before she got to the market. She had got herself to Ghana easily enough but could she get herself back to England and was it what she really wanted.

The cassava was sprouting, a filigree of green against the red earth, and the pawpaw tree was almost as tall as herself with a long spindly stem, a bouquet of leaves at the top and two small green fruits, the size of walnuts nestling there. Sometimes Grandmother followed her out to the farm, aware of her restlessness, wanting her to settle in Wanwangeri more than she had ever wanted anything, this child of Mante she had never thought to see, this gift for her old age.

Grandmother scolded her less now, recognised a stub-born streak like her own under Comfort's ready smile, her willingness to please, and loving her the more for it. She studied her needs and whims every way she could. Hadn't she given her a new-thatched hut of her own before the customary time, and two stools and a new sleeping mat and countless freedoms not allowed to the other children in the compound. That very day Comfort had gone out with her trading basket without asking, knotting the money in the top of her cloth as if it was her own. A been-to child was not like other children. Mante had never been the same, had never fully returned. What he owed to his mother for his education, what he owed to his sisters for the education of their children, was clear enough in the bright Ghanaian sunlight, but the shivering English fog had dimmed Mante's eyes for ever and made him indifferent to the obligations custom had laid down.

On the seventh day of Ama's close confinement, Comfort was kept busy in the compound all day, preparing the abomu and groundnut stew with Esi while Ata dressed Ama's hair ready for her *out-dooring*. There would be presents from everybody, Comfort flicked through her trading basket and wondered what to give, soap and talcum powder didn't seem enough for a sister's outdooring. On the eighth day there was an expectant hush and then a cry of joy as Ama appeared from her hut. Everybody clapped and the little ones jumped and shouted, 'Ama has come back to us.'

Ama smiled shyly. Her hair had been braided into a symmetrical pattern of partings all over her head and she wore a new cloth with golden yellow twisting lines on a black background. She blinked like some small animal emerging from a hibernating burrow as she stepped out of the dark hut where she had been for so long and sat in the middle of the compound to receive her presents. First Obodai, her father, came with two cloths, then Ata with a shining saucepan, Grandmother with a carved stool, Esi with a plastic bucket. Then it was Comfort's turn and as she laid the red handbag on Ama's lap, there was a little murmur of satisfaction. 'Very fine handbag. Red as the hibiscus flower,' they murmured and Ama's eyes widened as she stroked the smooth sides. Hadn't she always covetted the red handbag. Such things were hard to come by in Wanwangeri.

Visitors began to arrive from all round the village with good wishes and gifts for Ama. Bowls and saucepans, stools and cloths, everything she would need for her new adult life, enough soap to last three years, the gifts piled

up round her. All the visitors were given food and drink and Esi and Comfort and Tawia were busy all day. Late in the evening Comfort helped Ama to carry the mountain of gifts into her hut and stack them round the walls. Ama was friendly then and the two of them giggled and talked almost like before. But not quite.

After Ama was out-doored, Comfort returned to Akwapawa market. It was marvellous to be back. 'Aye-aye, Comfort, greetings, Comfort,' the market mammies called looking up from their baskets. 'Comfort, will you mind my stall? Comfort, will you write my letter?'

'Soon,' Comfort called back, arranging the cloths on Grandmother's stall in a round daisy-shape, each bolt a different petal. It had never been done that way before, Esi said, doubtful until Comfort sold twelve metres of cloth.

'Hey, Comfort,' the book-man called as she wandered across the lorry park in the late afternoon. He was washing the lorry and the motto, 'Dry Leaf Fall', shone white as teeth on the green bonnet. 'Have a biscuit, Comfort?'

Comfort sat on the lorry step where Esi could not see her and untied her diary. 'If I don't go back soon I shall never go back,' she wrote biting her biscuit, 'because I have already missed school for yonks and forgotten everything and Grandmother wants me to stay for always because I write better than anybody else in the compound and add figures quicker and help her with the lorry and because I'm her granddaughter, child of Mante, and her eyes and ears and all that stuff and it's ace looking after the stall and shouting out loud and doing what I like and magic trading for myself and bringing something home and not going to school which

I never liked all that much and I've got my own hut now which is the best thing in the world and my own grandmother wanting me to stay so much which is the other best thing in the world.'

Comfort looked up then and shouted at a woman passing, 'Buy my soap, pretty lady, this soap will make your skin as soft and sweet as frangipani.' The book-man let out a high pitched snort of laughter at such cheek but the woman tossed her head and did not stop and Comfort went back to her diary.

'I like it in Wanwangeri with drumming and dancing every day and pink dust flying and feast days too, so nearly every day is a party and when Bolo died, which was because of spirits or ghosts or because Obodai's other wife was jealous of such a beautiful child (nobody here reckons much on germs) and everybody cried because everybody was feeling the same thing all together and everybody cries much more than England and they laugh and joke much more too and the Chief in Akwapawa settles all quarrels and everybody has to keep the custom which is lots and lots of rules but everybody here belongs to everybody and everybody lives every day as it comes and every week as it comes and nobody thinks about tomorrow or next year much and that's the difference but my roots are in England.'

When Comfort got back from the market there was a curtain of plastic ribbon just like Grandmother's hanging at the door of her hut instead of a sack. The red and blue and green ribbons parted as the children darted through, letting the bright bands drag across their faces.

'Aye-aye, it is hard to get such things nowadays, kalabule, black market,' Grandmother said watching Comfort.

'Thank you, it is nice,' Comfort said putting her trading basket at the back of her hut. She sat on her sleeping mat. The ribbons flickered prettily against the evening sky but Comfort did not notice.

'Who is that boy at the compound gate?' Grandmother called from her stool later in the evening. She had been irritated by the flatness of Comfort's tone, her lack of gratitude, she was still irritated. Was there no pleasing the child. The drumming had started but Ata had promised to do Comfort's hair, parting it all over her head in segments like a cantaloupe melon. Ama had not joined the dancing either, she would wait with Comfort, she said, but now she stood at the compound gate whispering softly.

'It is Preko,' Ata said. 'He asks if he can visit Ama. He asks if his father can visit us to talk of family matters.'

'Aye-aye, Preko,' Grandmother sighed. 'I remember Preko's first out-dooring at eight days old. His is a respectable and hard-working family which keeps the customs. We will talk to his father.'

'Preko's family has more land than the others who want to visit Ama,' Ata observed.

'Is Ama going to get married already then?' Comfort asked.

'Maybe,' Ata said tugging at a tail of her hair and binding it round with cotton. 'When it has all been agreed. She cooks and knows well the skills a wife needs.'

'Soon it will be Comfort's turn to find a husband,' Esi said slyly. 'Who will we find to marry, Comfort?'

'A been-to boy,' Ata said laughing. 'Kwaku's nephew, Okoto, is studying in England right now but in two years time he will be back and looking for a been-to wife.'

'But I don't even know if I like him,' Comfort protested.

'Like? Of course you must like such a nice boy,' Ata scolded. 'Sit still, Comfort, how can I do your hair if you fidget so?'

'Go and show your grandmother,' Ata said giving her a little push when the hair was finished. Comfort ran her fingers along the partings, feeling her head strangely tight and the air cold at the back of her neck. Grandmother dozed on her stool under the pressure lamp, flying insects fluttered against its bright sides and termite wings lay on Grandmother's shoulders and lap. Sleeping she looked sad and very old, made of gnarled wood like the figurehead of some ancient ship.

'Grandmother,' Comfort whispered. 'Grandmother, my hair is done.'

'What?' Grandmother's eyes started open but for a second she stared at Comfort as if she didn't know her and her eyes glittered with tears. 'Aye-aye, Comfort, they have done your hair just as they did mine at your age. You look well, my Comfort, praise to Onyame who sent you.'

'Grandmother ....' Comfort swallowed, Comfort Jones, you've a long way to go. She had to say it now or she would never say it. She had to say it loud and clear. 'Grandmother I don't want to stay here. I want to go back.'

'Back to Mante?' Grandmother muttered and her face seemed to shrivel.

'Back to England,' Comfort said and once she had said it she knew it was true and she said it again. 'I want to go back to Granny in England.'

'Never,' Grandmother said and her stick swung up knocking the pressure lamp and setting it swinging so the compound rocked like a see-saw. 'Never, never, never,' she shrieked and outside the drumming stopped. 'A child belongs to her family and the family belongs to the child. Mante gave you to me and here you stay.'

'But I am not a present,' Comfort whispered quaking at Grandmother's anger. Her voice stuck in her throat like a cork wedged in a bottle and then burst free. 'I do not belong to you, I belong to myself.'

11

Grandmother's anger had erupted like a volcano but a
volcano erupts and is spent and Grandmother's anger
went on and on. She stayed in her hut for several days
but even then the low mutter of her voice followed
Comfort everywhere. Hadn't she spent her life-blood for
her son's schooling and what had come of it but a rash
marriage contracted without sense or caution and a
wilful child reared without proper respect. Only Onyame
knew how her family had disappointed and abused her.
Her voice droning on, cast a blight on the whole
compound so even the wind in the palm trees above
sounded like a sad moaning. The children sat in their
corner, too dispirited to play, keeping a wide-eyed watch
on her hut.

'Can I go to my farm?' Comfort asked. It was Ama
and Ata who went to the market in Akwapawa now.

'Go to your farm? Aye-aye, there is nothing but
trouble from you, Comfort,' Esi said. 'You must ask your
grandmother.'

'Grandmother,' Comfort called and her legs were
jelly-like as she touched the plastic ribbons at Grandmother's doorway and they quivered in the bright sun.
But it was no good being frightened, Comfort thought,
'Fear Eats the Soul' was the motto on the lorry they had

taken North. 'Grandmother, can I go to my farm today?'

'Go, go, go,' Grandmother cried. 'Tell the ancestors how you have misbehaved, water Onyame's earth with your tears and sorrowing and beg him to change your wicked heart.'

'Yes, Grandmother,' Comfort mumbled. 'Sorry, sorry, sorry,' she added as she picked up her hoe. She had wounded her grandmother's feelings and she was sorry for that. But how could she be sorry because she wanted to return to England, Comfort thought. You did not *decide* to want, you just wanted. She walked toward her farm with her basket on her head. She took the basket everywhere. There was always the possibility of a small trade, a few pesawas to be made and knotted into her cloth, the solid lumps of coins pressed against her waist but nowhere else was so safe.

The two pawpaw fruits were as big as apples now. Comfort gazed at them a moment and then doubled back, slipping between the grey trunks of palm-trees, straight as pencils, until she reached Sika's compound and went inside. Sika, the headman, was potter to the village too and a deep resonating rumble came from the hut in front of her. Comfort stood at the doorway and Sika's eyes flicked uneasily towards her but his hands, slippery with wet clay, worked on at the wheel which his nephew and apprentice turned with a handle.

'Greetings, wise one,' Comfort whispered as her eyes got used to the dimness inside the hut.

'I was expecting you,' he said. 'There is argument in your compound, who can keep their troubles secret in Wanwangeri?'

'I want to go back to England,' Comfort said tracing a line in the dust with her toe. It would be better manners

to proceed more slowly, she knew, admiring his skill as a
potter, his reputation for settling disputes, the good looks
and health of his small son who stood in the doorway
beside her with a string of black and white beads round
his waist. But her voice was wobbly already and if she
didn't state her purpose at once she might not be able to
state it at all.

'You want to go back to England?' Sika repeated
dipping his hand into the pot of water beside him but
keeping his eyes on the wheel. Comfort watched too as
the clay rose and opened under his hands like a huge
grey flower. Suddenly the wheel stopped, a knife flashed
deftly severing the pot from its base. 'And what does
your grandmother say?'

'She wants me to stay,' Comfort muttered, catching
the eyes of the apprentice, an older son of Ata who lived
in his father's compound, her brother though they had
hardly spoken. Everybody was related to everybody in
Wanwangeri. 'She wants me to stay forever.'

'Then the matter is settled,' Sika said taking another clay ball from the pile beside him. 'How can a child disobey the wishes of her grandmother? Did your father not send you to Wanwangeri?' The clay hit the centre of the wheel with a decisive slap. 'These are difficult times,' he said as the wheel began to rumble round again. 'Prices rising faster than ant-hills, should your family also be troubled by a disobedient child?' He glanced towards the doorway and the small boy felt his father's eye and scampered away. 'Go back to your grandmother, Comfort. The Chief himself would tell you the same thing. Do you hear me child?'

'I hear you, wise one,' Comfort said.

She walked across the centre of Wanwangeri then. Somehow she had to find her way back to England and if the path ran through the Chief's compound at Akwapawa that was where she had to go. And she had to go at once. A little girl came skipping towards her with an empty bucket in her hand.

'Greetings, Comfort, where are you going? Can I come with you?'

'Greetings, Yoyoe,' Comfort said walking on down the path. 'Sorry, I am going a long way and you have water to fetch.'

At the edge of the village Comfort looked back at the scatter of brown-fenced compounds under the palm-trees, blue smoke rising, hearing the chink of an axe, a distant chanting, 'Four fours are sixteen, four fives are twenty . . . .'

A hen and three chicks came out of the bush and pecked round her bare feet and ran on. Comfort turned with a sudden choking in her throat. How could she go without saying goodbye? How could she say goodbye when Grandmother was so angry? But now as she walked along the path her legs felt stiff, as if they agreed with Grandmother and Sika and Onyame that she ought to stay, and yet every step was carrying her slowly but steadily away from Wanwangeri.

Comfort had never walked the path to Akwapawa by herself. Birds fluttered suddenly from the scrubby thorn bushes and her hand tightened on her hoe. Beyond the trees the heat shimmered from the ground like red lakes and a faint drumming throbbed in the air. Were the drums sending a message to Akwapawa ahead of her, Comfort wondered, or was it just the frightened beat of her own heart.

By the time she reached the town it was cooler and the market was busy. Comfort made her way to the Chief's compound which had a breeze-block wall round it, a floor of dusty concrete and huts roofed with corrugated iron, gleaming silvery in the sun. The Chief sat on a stool shaded by a huge umbrella, pink and gold and green, listening to complaints and arguments with his advisor beside him. One or two heads turned curiously as Comfort joined the line of people waiting but if they had received any message of a runaway girl from the talking drums they gave no sign.

'You are from Wanwangeri?' the Chief said when it was her turn at last. He was old but his eyes were bright, brilliant jet specks between crinkled lids. He wore a blue and white crown on his head and a gold chain around his neck and an air of intelligent and unquestioned authority.

'Yes,' whispered Comfort staring at the ground. How did he know she came from Wanwangeri unless he had magic powers. 'I came from England seven moons ago and I want to go back to my grandmother there. But Grandmother here wants me to stay.' Comfort sighed gustily.

'How can a child know what is best for her?' the Chief snorted turning to his adviser. 'How can this girl from Wanwangeri have a grandmother in England?'

'It is possible,' his adviser said diffidently, unwilling to commit himself either way. 'The father of this girl was married in England, they say.'

'I am Comfort Kwatey-Jones,' Comfort said, fixing her eyes on the blue and white crown to avoid the intensity of the Chief's gaze. She could just make out a small picture, a sailor's head on the front of it and then she saw that the crown, blue and white and neat as it was, was composed of hundreds of cigarette packets, flattened and laid one upon the other like the scales of a fish. The jaunty humour of such ingenuity was reassuring and gave Comfort the courage to meet his eyes.

'What is this England to you, Comfort Kwatey-Jones?'

the Chief said. 'The English are as cold as their climate, they tell me, and black people are not welcomed there as guests are welcomed here. "Share meal with friend, rich in fortune." So why do you want to leave our sunshine? What can there be in England for a black girl like you?'

'The girl is sky-sky, touched in the head,' the adviser suggested.

'I just want to,' Comfort said slowly, thinking hard and dream-seeing London now. 'People can be mean and sometimes they say rude words and how long are you stopping and things like that. But people can be nice too, people like Miss Trilby, my teacher, for instance, and Mrs Mace and Lettie, she's my friend, and Carmen, she's my other friend, and Granny and Grandad and I want to go to school and there's lots of schools and England is where I come from.'

'Ghana is where you come from,' the Chief said sternly. 'How can you leave your family here, a child belongs to her family?'

'Only slaves belong to people,' Comfort said. 'I belong to myself.'

'This girl is disobedient and ill-mannered, no good can

come from such wild talk,' the adviser said. But the Chief held up his hand for silence and looked at Comfort for a long time. His eyes, bright as lasers, seemed to see right inside her mind, mesmerising, making a softness, such a weariness that Comfort wanted no more talk, no more argument. She would do just what the Chief said. If he told her to go back to Wanwangeri she would go at once and stay for ever.

'The eagle that is reared as a chicken will still be an eagle,' the Chief said at length. 'Let the girl take her eagle blood back to England.'

'Will you tell my grandmother?' Comfort said. 'I shall come back, I promise to come back.' But the Chief had closed his eyes and the adviser was already dismissing her with a jerk of his head.

It was dark when Comfort reached the lorry park beside the market. Ata and Ama had already left for Wanwangeri and the other cloth stalls were closed too but the food stalls were still trading. A pressure lamp hung above each one, making a circle of light, a bright white dandelion-clock in the darkness.

Comfort bought roasted plantains, biting through the burnt black shell to the hot and sweet-sour succulence and staying out of sight in the shadows, watching and waiting. Everybody knew Grandmother and news travelled fast when the drums talked but nobody came looking for Comfort. 'Dry Leaf Fall' shone white on the bonnet of Grandmother's lorry and Comfort waited until the very last moment when the book-man shouted and banged up the back and then she ran.

'Hey wait, is there room for me?'

'Aye-aye, Comfort, of course there is room for your grandmother's granddaughter,' the book-man said letting the flap down so she could scramble in. 'And where is your grandmother sending you this evening?'

'South,' said Comfort swallowing rapidly.

'South,' said the book-man savouring the word like a delicate morsel in his mouth. 'How far is that?'

'A long way,' said Comfort.

The lorry moved out and along the street and lights from shops and stalls fell on the faces round her. Market women with children sleeping on their laps and baskets of fruit beside them. There was a burst of talk as the lorry left Akwapawa but many had already waited a long time and silence fell as they left the town and moved into the darkness of the bush.

Comfort sat with the basket on her knees. Talcum powder and soap, she had presents for everybody at Hillside now. It was not right in Ghana to arrive without presents. She had money in her cloth and her diary round her neck and she let the pages flitter against her fingers in the darkness. The days of her life. She had had to leave everything else, the striped suitcase and what was left of her clothes. It was best to travel light.

Soon there were lights again and the smell of food cooking and the market women round her woke, yawned and disappeared towards their huts.

'Where are you going to stay, Comfort?' the book-man asked, he was looking at her curiously now, sensing something amiss. 'Do you want to sleep at my place?'

'Thank you,' said Comfort.

'Share a meal with friends, rich in fortune,' the book-man said cheerily and Comfort smiled reading his thoughts. How grateful her grandmother would be if he took her back. That night she ate with his children and slept on a sleeping mat beside them but in the morning she woke early and slipped out. Comfort was going south.

It was evening again when she reached Hillside Estate. There were lights in the servant's quarters and for a moment she stood in the darkness, silent under the stars, feeling the dew-cold earth under her feet and watching as John came down the steps and hung something on the washing line and went in again. The murmur of voices.

Mante sat on the back veranda, smiling down at something concealed by the low veranda wall.

'Who is there?' he said staring into the darkness as a twig snapped, startled as Comfort ran up the steps. 'Comfort?' He jumped up and folded his arms round her just as he had done that first day at Accra airport seven moths ago. 'What are you doing here, Comfort, wandering in the darkness like a ghost?'

'I want to go back to England,' Comfort said breathlessly.

Mante drew back then and now she could see what he had been watching. A young girl sat on a low stool giving the baby, Jeo, his bottle. Jeo's eyes turned curiously towards Comfort and he dropped the teat from his mouth with a squelchy rush of bubbles and smiled a wide milky smile.

'Let him feed,' Mante said softly. 'Let my fine son feed and grow strong.'

'Where is Efua?' Comfort said.

'She has gone back to work, air-hostess for Ghana Airways.' Mante said glancing towards the night sky. 'She flies all over the place, Efua is a modern woman. This is her young cousin, Peace, who lives with us and takes care of Jeo.'

'Greetings, Peace,' Comfort nodded.

'And why is my daughter, Comfort, coming out of the darkness like a bush child with no sandals even,' Mante said. 'And what of your grandmother who has wanted to see you since you were born? You belong to your grandmother now.'

'Gradually a chick will grow to eat by itself,' Comfort said. 'And I don't belong to anybody.' There was drumming out in the darkness. Comfort told Mante all that had happened, her farm and market stall at Akwa-pawa, Ama's out-dooring and the death of Bolo, Sika and her visit to the Chief. Mante listened quietly and when she had finished he fetched a pile of letters. There were letters from Granny and Grandad and postcards from Lettie in Penfold and Carmen in London and Mrs Mace. Peace took Jeo away to his cot and Comfort and Mante sat on the veranda.

'And how can I pay to send you back to England?' her father said. Mante who was brilliant and tricky too. 'Our two salaries are not enough, don't I work all day and taxi half the night?'

'I have money,' Comfort said and she untied the knots in her cloth and dropped the contents on the table, notes and coins, cedis from her trading and letter-writing, pounds from the red handbag.

'So much money!' her father whispered as the money piled up. 'You are your grandmother's granddaughter that is certain.'

'We have the same name and the same spirit,' Comfort said and now she understood the message of the drums. 'Comfort Kwatey-Jones, Comfort Kwatey-Jones, you've a long way to go.'

12

'Tonight is my last night and tomorrow is my birthday and I'm going to England,' Comfort wrote sitting at the end of her bed. The veranda light had been left on for Mante and she could just see to write while she waited. Jeo gave a little whimpering sound in his sleep and Comfort got up and stood beside the white cot, tucking the flannelette sheet over his shoulder and feeling the slight roughness of his head, the tiny sprouting hairs under her fingers. His lips were crinkled like a mushroom round his thumb, his cheek pressed flat against the blue organdie pillowcase.

'Jeo, Jeo, my little brother.' Comfort whispered, rocking the cot and longing for him to wake so she could pick him up and hold him tight against her chest but Jeo slept on.

The girl, Peace, lay in a camp-bed beside the cot with her cloth wrapped tight round her like a cocoon. She stayed all day and night with Jeo, sleeping when he slept, eating when he ate and smiling when he smiled, their lives entwined like tendrils of honeysuckle. Cicadas whirred in the bushes under the window and drums throbbed in the darkness far away. 'I expect Granny will be quite angry that I *forgot* to write for so long,' Comfort wrote but she did not mind so much now about people getting angry. 'A year ago today Miss Trilby gave me and Carmen silver stars for our geography project and it was sausages and chips for dinner and pink trifle. Yuck.'

There was an almost full moon, ringed with mist Cool night air filtered in through the mosquito-netted window and Paddington stirred gently in its flow. Comfort heard the car slide into the garage and Mante's footsteps, the click of the study light and she crept along the veranda. He sat with a clean sheet of paper in front of him. However late he was he worked on his book.

'Comfort, so you are leaving me?' he said leaning back in his chair. 'You are going back to England.'

'Yes,' said Comfort.

'I suppose it is best,' Mante sighed. 'You are to go to school in Folkestone your granny writes. You must work hard at that school, you must do well at that school, I shall expect top marks.' Mante put his arm round her and smiled ruefully. Such words had been said to him in his childhood, planted like millet in his head and taken root. 'Nothing worth having is won easily in this life,' he added.

'I shall miss you and little Jeo,' Comfort said softly, but staring into the velvet darkness it was Wanwangeri she could see, Grandmother who had wanted her to stay so much.

'Perhaps you can visit in a year or two,' Mante said. 'Never forget that we share the same spirit. Aye-aye, a child should grow up with her family.' He rocked in his chair then just as Grandmother had rocked in sadness. 'How can I let my own child go?'

'I shall write,' Comfort said, sorry for his sadness and at that instant sorry she was going. 'And I promise to come back.'

'Yes, come back, Comfort,' Mante said. 'There is no sadness like a child lost. Here,' he opened the drawer of his desk. 'Your mother gave me this ring and it's right that it should come to you.'

'I'll wear it round my neck,' Comfort said holding the plain gold circle in her palm. 'It will keep me safe like the amulet.'

'You get pulled apart belonging to two places,' Mante said. 'Don't let them pull you apart, Comfort, England and Africa.'

'The stranger has big eyes but does not see what is happening,' Comfort said and Mante laughed then, his deep rumbling laugh.

'You're not a stranger, Comfort, besides the stranger often sees more than the family at the hearth. England and Ghana struggle in your heart, just as the old and the new ways struggle in all of us. But you have the heart of an eagle, Comfort, you're a modern girl, brave and strong.'

'And isn't Efua a modern woman?' Comfort said.

'Ancient and modern like the hymnbook. Aye-aye, our Jeo is well-protected with antiseptic and vitamins and magic and fetish priests too. The world is changing fast,' Mante said. The whites of his eyes were pink now, working in the office all day and driving a taxi at night, no wonder he was tired, Comfort thought. 'Creative tension, they call it, creative tension keeps me working on this book.' He levelled the edges of the blank pages together and put them into his desk drawer. 'But not tonight.' The drumming was louder now, coming clearly across the dark plain from the shanty village. 'Drumming is Africa,' Mante said softly, 'Africa is we.'

'You'll write to me won't you?' Comfort said. Tears

were thundering inside her louder than the drumming but her eyes stayed dry. What was the use of crying which only stuffed up your nose and made your head ache? Beside they might make her stay if she cried. She was sad now but going back to England was what she wanted.

'Many happy returns, many happy returns, Comfort,' Granny said hugging Comfort tight and just behind her Grandad polished the end of his nose with his hanky so it shone like a cherry.

'Can't call you little now, can we, twelve years old?'

'I should think not indeed,' Granny said straightening her new cyclamen hat. 'All your presents are at home ready.'

'Presents?' said Comfort wonderingly, her head still full of engines roaring. 'Home?'

'Back at Smithy Cottage,' Granny said. 'Bless me, the child has forgotten her birthday, whatever next?'

'It's my best day, the best day in the whole lot is June 12th,' Grandad said.

'Forgetting your own birthday,' Granny said fizzing like a sherbet stick with the excitement of it all. 'You'll have to do better than that, Comfort. When I was your age lots of girls of twelve were earning their own living, straight into service, kitchen maids at twelve.'

'I know,' said Comfort catching Grandad's wink.

'And whatever are you wearing?' Granny said diving into the zip bag that Grandad was carrying. 'Good job I brought your cardigan, I only hope it fits after all this time.'

'It's nice and warm,' Comfort said, pulling the dark-green cardigan over her balloon-patterned cloth. 'Thanks.'

'Fits like a glove,' Granny said triumphant. 'You've changed Comfort, thinner altogether, and what ever have they done to your hair?'

'I like it like this,' Comfort said patting the tiny braids that Ata had made in Wanwangeri. I shall keep it like this, I've washed it like this twice.'

'Thank goodness for small mercies,' Granny said.

In the train Granny talked and Comfort looked out at the greys and browns of London, back gardens with swings and sandpits and then the lush green of Kent. England was always the same but not quite the same. Would a blue sky always be as blue as Paddington's coat in Hillside Estate and would the rhythmic clank of the train always sound like the drumming in Wanwangeri, Comfort wondered, hugging the bundle on her knees.

'That Lettie Stamp's been round asking twice,' Granny was saying. 'Trust her to smell birthday cake a mile off.'

'Birthday cake?' Comfort said.

'Shan't do it every year mind, all that icing is too much fiddle,' Granny said. 'And you've got to look forward now, Comfort. Get on with things. Next week we're going over to Folkestone to see the headmistress and get your uniform and then we're leaving you at school. You'll be back for the weekends of course.'

'School?' Comfort said aghast, trying to turn a fraction into a decimal in her head but turning it instead into cedis and pesawas. 'It's a whole year since I went to school, I bet I've forgotten everything.'

'Then you'll have to work hard to catch up,' Granny said. 'Hard work never hurt anybody. *Wear out don't rust out*. Whatever have you done with that nice case I gave you with your initials, paid a nice price too?'

'I left it in Wanwangeri,' Comfort said looking out at orchards but seeing the case against the smooth red wall of her hut. She didn't want to explain about the Chief at Akwapawa and running away. She didn't want to talk about all that happened and she didn't think Granny and Grandad would ask. Were the pawpaw on her farm as big as grapefruit now, Comfort wondered.

It was late when the taxi slid up the lane and squares of amber light shone from the cottages round. Bats swooped in the twilight from the Norman tower and children stood still as statues in the shadows under the beech tree. Comfort heard their whispers like a breeze stirring the leaves. 'It's Comfort, Comfort's back.'

And then silence.

'I knew we should be tired,' Granny said and if she heard the whispers too she gave no sign. 'I left the table all laid ready, won't take a moment to heat up the soup.'

'Can I open my presents now?' Comfort said. She unwrapped the crisp patterned paper, listening for the sounds outside. There was a small work-basket with needles and cottons and a blue letter-writing case fitted out with paper and envelopes.

'Practical presents,' Granny said. 'I always give practical presents. And what do you think of your birthday cake?' The cake on the dining room table was far from practical. A pale lilac cake with a tiny crinoline lady standing in the middle and the cake belling out round her.

'Oh, it's magic, gay as a pineapple,' Comfort said and she flung her arms round Granny. 'I never had such a fine-fine home-made birthday cake before.'

'Tch, tch, it's nothing special, child,' Granny said. 'Just a light sponge mixture and two layers of butter icing. Oh, those silly children,' she added as a shrill squeal came from the other side of the hedge.

'Can't they have some cake?' Comfort said.

'I didn't make this lovely cake for children screaming on the green,' Granny said sharply. 'Letting them play outside at this time of night. Take your presents upstairs, Comfort, while I just heat the soup.'

In the attic bedroom Comfort stretched and touched the ceiling with one finger. She could do that easily now, she must be at least an inch taller. She sat at her dressing-table and undid her bundle. The diary. It was time now and she took a deep breath and pulled out the paper clip, leaving a rusty mark on the page. *Margaret*, she had written on that day almost a year ago and ringed it round and round with pencil.

'Margaret,' Comfort said feeling the gold ring against her neck. It was a long time since she had looked at herself in a mirror and now she smiled at herself, a full wide smile, and then laughed just as Margaret laughed. She did look different, Granny had said she did, she looked more like Margaret. And she didn't care so much what people said any more and she didn't care so much when people got angry any more, she had an eagle's heart and friends everywhere too like Margaret, Carmen in Brixton and Ama in Wanwangeri and Winnie and Big Man in Accra and Lettie in Penfold.

It was quite dark now and the full moon was ringed with mist just as it had been the night before in Ghana and the swallows were back under the eaves. Comfort heard the latch on the church gate as the Rector locked up, his footsteps receding down the lane and the distant bleat of sheep. The green was quiet but as she stared at the deep black under the beech tree she thought she saw something move and then a voice called, 'Lettie, come in do.'

'Lettie,' Comfort whispered launching the words into the darkness like little boats. 'Lettie where are you?'

But Granny was calling from downstairs. 'Dinner's ready, Comfort.'

'Shall I light the candles?' Comfort said carrying the cake to the deep window-sill in the thickness of the cottage wall. The match scratched on the box and the twelve candles on the crinoline skirt bloomed into little flames. Grandad put out the light.

'What a picture,' Granny said spooning oxtail soup and smiling.

'Can I have the lady after?' Comfort said, thinking of the reindeer and sledge and a christmas long ago.

'You'll have to take care of it, mind,' Granny said. 'It's real bone china.'

'Corned beef and salad,' Grandad said collecting up the plates. 'And then cake for afters, seems a shame to cut it just for us?' The meal was almost finished when the gate flung back and footsteps scampered on the path and bubbles of giggle burst all round the dark garden.

'It's those children all over my garden, all over my roses,' Granny said getting up. 'Shoo, shoo.'

'Only natural with Comfort back?' Grandad said. 'They want to see our Comfort.'

Comfort opened the front door and walked down the path like a sleep-walker with the cake in her arms. The twelve candles guttered in the night air but did not go out.

'You got back then,' Lettie said, her eyes shining green

as grapes in the candlelight. 'Didn't know you were coming back, did I?'

'Neither did I?' Comfort said. 'Want some birthday cake?'

'You bet,' said Lettie.

'Me too,' said Colin and Betty and Ruth and Dave and Carol and Joy and little Freddie Bone. There were nine children in the garden now and more coming across the green in dressing-gowns as if the candles had called them back from sleep. They stood round the cake as Comfort set it on the grass. Even the Watkins children, smiling clumsily and pausing at the gate, half-expecting somebody might tell them to go away, but nobody did.

'You've got to blow this whole lot out, all the twelve in one blow,' Lettie said, 'then you can wish.'

Comfort blew. A long blow that took all her breath, her face moving round the cake and round again like the sun round the earth, until the last candle winked and died. There was a smell of candlewax in the darkness. Grandad fetched a knife from the dining room and Granny switched on the porch light.

'That's a lovely little old cake that is,' Lettie said with a quick glance at Granny as Comfort pressed the knife down. 'Best cake, prettiest cake I ever did see.'

'Just sponge and butter-icing,' Comfort said surprising herself with Granny's voice. But it wasn't really surprising, she thought, as she cut the cake into slices, because she was partly made of Mante and Margaret and Grandmother in Wanwangeri and Granny in Penfold, and partly of everything that had happened to her, but the rest was unique, *Comfort herself*.

'What did you want to come back here for?' Colin said with his hair falling over his eyes and his mouth full of cake.

'Stop asking silly questions,' Lettie said. 'This is where she belongs isn't it? Comfort Kwatey-Jones lives in Penfold, Kent, England, the World.'

ALSO IN

HEINEMANN NEW WINDMILLS

General Editors: Anne and Ian Serraillier

Chinua Achebe Things Fall Apart
Douglas Adams The Hitchhiker's Guide to the Galaxy
Vivien Alcock The Cuckoo Sister; The Monster Garden; The Trial of Anna Cotman; A Kind of Thief
Margaret Atwood The Handmaid's Tale
J G Ballard Empire of the Sun
Nina Bawden The Witch's Daughter; A Handful of Thieves; Carrie's War; The Robbers; Devil by the Sea; Kept in the Dark; The Finding; Keeping Henry; Humbug
E R Braithwaite To Sir, With Love
John Branfield The Day I Shot My Dad
F Hodgson Burnett The Secret Garden
Ray Bradbury The Golden Apples of the Sun; The Illustrated Man
Betsy Byars The Midnight Fox; Goodbye, Chicken Little; The Pinballs
Victor Canning The Runaways; Flight of the Grey Goose
Ann Coburn Welcome to the Real World
Hannah Cole Bring in the Spring
Jane Leslie Conly Racso and the Rats of NIMH
Robert Cormier We All Fall Down
Roald Dahl Danny, The Champion of the World; The Wonderful Story of Henry Sugar; George's Marvellous Medicine; The BFG; The Witches; Boy; Going Solo; Charlie and the Chocolate Factory; Matilda
Anita Desai The Village by the Sea
Charles Dickens A Christmas Carol; Great Expectations
Peter Dickinson The Gift; Annerton Pit; Healer
Berlie Doherty Granny was a Buffer Girl
Gerald Durrell My Family and Other Animals
J M Falkner Moonfleet
Anne Fine The Granny Project
Anne Frank The Diary of Anne Frank
Leon Garfield Six Apprentices
Jamila Gavin The Wheel of Surya
Adele Geras Snapshots of Paradise

Graham Greene The Third Man and The Fallen Idol; Brighton Rock

Thomas Hardy The Withered Arm and Other Wessex Tales

Rosemary Harris Zed

L P Hartley The Go-Between

Ernest Hemingway The Old Man and the Sea; A Farewell to Arms

Nat Hentoff Does this School have Capital Punishment?

Nigel Hinton Getting Free; Buddy; Buddy's Song

Minfong Ho Rice Without Rain

Anne Holm I Am David

Janni Howker Badger on the Barge; Isaac Campion

Linda Hoy Your Friend Rebecca

Barbara Ireson (Editor) In a Class of Their Own

Jennifer Johnston Shadows on Our Skin

Toeckey Jones Go Well, Stay Well

James Joyce A Portrait of the Artist as a Young Man

Geraldine Kaye Comfort Herself; A Breath of Fresh Air

Clive King Me and My Million

Dick King-Smith The Sheep-Pig

Daniel Keyes Flowers for Algernon

Elizabeth Laird Red Sky in the Morning; Kiss the Dust

D H Lawrence The Fox and The Virgin and the Gypsy; Selected Tales

Harper Lee To Kill a Mockingbird

Julius Lester Basketball Game

Ursula Le Guin A Wizard of Earthsea

C Day Lewis The Otterbury Incident

David Line Run for Your Life; Screaming High

Joan Lingard Across the Barricades; Into Exile; The Clearance; The File on Fraulein Berg

Penelope Lively The Ghost of Thomas Kempe

Jack London The Call of the Wild; White Fang

Bernard Mac Laverty Cal; The Best of Bernard Mac Laverty

Margaret Mahy The Haunting; The Catalogue of The Universe

Jan Mark Do You Read Me? Eight Short Stories

James Vance Marshall Walkabout

Somerset Maugham The Kite and Other Stories

Michael Morpurgo Waiting for Anya; My Friend Walter; The War of Jenkins' Ear

How many have you read?